"I'm going to the police station,"

Darcy told Molly. "Do you want me to ask your mom to come up and be with you?"

Molly shook her head. "And don't tell my parents what happened, either. They're still trying to get over the other accident. I don't want them to get upset all over again."

"Okay," Darcy agreed softly. She shut Molly's door and hurried downstairs and out to the van. Just as she was about to open the door on the driver's side, a light flashed in her head.

And she knew.

The person driving that car was the same person who had hit Molly.

Mesmerized, she stared into the distance, willing a picture of the person's face to come to her. But all she saw was darkness and fear.

Also by Cherie Bennett

The SUNSET ISLAND series

Sunset
After Dark

CHERIE BENNETT

SPLASH™

B

A BERKLEY / SPLASH BOOK

SUNSET AFTER DARK is an original publication of The Berkley Publishing Group. This work has never appeared before in book form.

SUNSET AFTER DARK

A Berkley Book / published by arrangement with General Licensing Company, Inc.

PRINTING HISTORY
Berkley edition / March 1993

ISBN: 0-425-13772-4

A BERKLEY BOOK ® TM 757,375
Berkley Books are published by The Berkley Publishing Group, 200 Madison Avenue, New York, New York 10016.
The name "BERKLEY" and the "B" logo are trademarks belonging to Berkley Publishing Corporation.

PRINTED IN THE UNITED STATES OF AMERICA

10 9 8 7 6 5 4 3 2 1

For my dad,
Bennett H. Berman,
who always believed in me

ONE

This is a day I'll remember my whole life, Darcy Laken thought as she looked down at the diploma the principal, Dr. Green, had just handed her. It was a perfect June afternoon, and her mother, father, three brothers, and two sisters were all sitting out there on the lawn watching her high school graduation. And the most exciting part was still to come.

"The Belinda Kramer Award for Athletic Excellence is an important tradition here at Kennedy High," the principal was saying from the podium.

This was it, the moment Darcy had been waiting for. Her heart beat double time in her chest. *Please let me win*, she prayed silently, her white-knuckled fingers clenched tightly around her diploma. *I've got to win.*

"As you know," Dr. Green continued, "Belinda Kramer was a student here at Kennedy High from 1971 until she graduated in 1975. And as you also know, Belinda made our school, our town, and our country proud when she won not one but two gold medals for swimming in the 1976 summer Olympics in Montreal, Canada. Tragically, Belinda died two short years later from bone cancer."

A sad murmur went through the crowd. Everyone in Portland knew this story as well as if Belinda Kramer had been a member of their own family. Darcy realized it was the stories she'd heard about Belinda that had made her want to become a diver in the first place.

"Belinda's family began a wonderful scholarship fund in her name, with the scholarship to be given every year to the best female athlete in the senior class here at Kennedy High," the principal continued. "But not only must the winner be the best athlete. She must also be a person of character and moral fiber, a young woman who upholds the very spirit of the Olympic games."

"It's you, I know it's you!" Suki Lamb, Darcy's best friend, whispered excitedly in

Darcy's ear. She grabbed Darcy's arm and squeezed it.

Darcy was too nervous even to answer Suki. The scholarship would mean so much to her. Even with the diving scholarship she'd been offered at the University of Maine, she still needed money for books, for food, for just plain living. No way could her parents afford to help her, much as they'd like to.

As Darcy closed her eyes even more tightly, willing the principal to call her name, all the years she'd spent perfecting her diving came rushing back to her, like a movie on fast-forward. The sacrifices her family had made, the hours upon hours at the pool diving again and again and again . . .

"And so it is with great pride," the principal's sonorous voice boomed, "that I announce the winner of the Belinda Kramer Award for Athletic Excellence, a scholarship in the amount of ten thousand dollars . . ."

Please let it be me. Please . . .

"Marianne Elizabeth Reed!"

Everyone applauded. Marianne and her friends squealed and hugged one another, then Marianne ran up to the podium.

But for Darcy Laken, time stopped.

Marianne Reed, the perky blond head-cheerleader and baton twirler, the daughter of the city council president, had won instead of her.

"You got ripped, Laken," Kenny Monroe snorted from the row behind Darcy. "Athletic excellence in baton twirling? Gimme a break!"

"God, Darcy, I'm so sorry," Suki said softly. "I just can't believe this happened."

"It's no biggie," Darcy said, clamping her jaw hard to prevent herself from crying. She felt as if everyone in the senior class was looking at her to see how she was taking it. Well, no way was she going to give them the satisfaction of seeing her cry. The last time she'd cried in front of those other students, she'd been fourteen years old, and she'd vowed then that she'd never, ever let it happen again. . . .

"No way am I wearing this, Mom," *fourteen-year-old Darcy stated, looking down at herself in the terrible shiny brown dress with the excruciating cap sleeves.*

It was the day before the first day of school. That summer Darcy and her family had moved from Bangor, where Darcy had grown up, to Portland, and Darcy wanted desperately to fit in in a new place. When the bank had foreclosed on their home, Darcy's uncle, who owned a lot of property, had offered them a dilapidated house in Portland rent-free. Darcy hated it, as did the rest of the family, but they tried to make the best of a really awful situation.

Darcy would be beginning the ninth grade—in high school at long last. The only good news about moving to Portland was that Darcy's intelligence and excellent grades had gotten her into the magnet school for the smartest kids in the city, Kennedy High. The brightest—and often wealthiest—kids in the city went to Kennedy. Darcy was so excited about it, she could hardly sleep at night. No more going to a school where kids actually brought weapons to school, where you took your life in your hands just trying to get from class to class. Everything would be different now.

Darcy was determined to be a great student, to look good, to fit in. She knew the first impression she made would be crucial. Just the night before she'd studied herself in the full-length mirror in the bathroom, trying to see what her new fellow classmates would see. Her long black hair was shiny and luxurious. Her violet eyes were thickly lashed—a little mascara would make them look even bigger. So far so good.

Then her eyes scanned her image from neck to feet, and she sighed deeply. How had she gotten so tall and so big so fast? She'd shot up two inches over the summer, and she'd already been the tallest girl in her class. Now she stood five feet nine inches in her stocking feet. And then there was her body. There was no way around it—she was big. Not fat—she could see she wasn't really fat. But just like her dad and her brothers, she had a big-boned, athletic body, and there was nothing she could do to change that.

Now that she'd grown so much, none of her school clothes from the year before fit anymore. Even if Kennedy High allowed kids to wear jeans—which it didn't—hers were now two inches too short. So her mother had gone out shopping for school clothes, and this thing was what she had brought home.

"It's a nice dress, honey," her mother said, brushing a piece of lint off the full skirt that came down to Darcy's shins.

"It's horrible and you know it," Darcy seethed. "I hate it. No one in high school dresses like this."

"Well, maybe I could jazz it up a little," her mother suggested, deep lines appearing between her brows. "Some fancy buttons, maybe."

"Fancy buttons?" Darcy screeched. How could her mother be so totally, completely out of it? "Look, forget it," she said, pulling the loathsome garment over her head. "We'll take it back and I'll go shopping with you for something decent." Darcy threw the dress on the couch. "You should have just let me go with you in the first place. Where did you get it, anyway?"

Her mother began to fiddle with the buttons on the front of her faded sweater— something she did whenever she was anxious. "I think we can fix up this dress, Darcy, really."

Darcy zipped up her too short jeans and stared at her mother. "We can't, Mom. Honest."

"Well, honey, I don't think we can return it," her mother said, fiddling even more anxiously with her buttons.

"Okay, so we'll exchange it," Darcy said. "Where'd you get it?"

"Well, um . . ." Darcy's mom began, her eyes not meeting Darcy's.

"It's okay if it's K Mart, Mom," Darcy said gently, buttoning her cotton blouse. Her mother knew Darcy hated it when she shopped at K Mart, but the clothes there were at least affordable.

"I got it at the Salvation Army," Darcy's mother said at last.

Darcy's fingers stopped on the last button of her shirt. "You what?"

This time her mother looked her right in the eye. "The Salvation Army," her mother repeated, holding her head high. "I didn't take you shopping with me because I didn't want you to feel embarrassed."

Darcy sat heavily on their worn sofa. "But . . ." she began.

"But nothing," her mother said firmly. She sat on the couch next to Darcy. "With your dad out of work and all the medical bills, things are real tight right now."

"I know," Darcy said in a low voice. Her father had had a stroke just three months earlier, and was now home from the hospital but bedridden. Even in the best of times her dad's job as an auto mechanic and her mom's job as a waitress had barely made ends meet for a family of seven. Now with her dad out of work, possibly forever, they got public assistance to supplement her mom's income. It was something Darcy hated even to think about.

"Everyone needed new shoes, and Dean had to have that dental work done," her mother said. "Well, we just can't afford more than this right now, Darcy." She took her daughter's hand. "I'm sorry."

Darcy saw the pain etched in her mother's eyes. She'd aged so much since her husband's stroke! Darcy threw her arms around her mother and hugged her fiercely. "It's okay, Mom," she said. "The dress isn't really that bad. A lot of kids wear clothes from second-hand shops. It's actually kind of cool."

Her mother's answering smile loosened the terrible tightening in Darcy's throat. She couldn't stand to see her mother upset. "I'll add a belt and stuff," Darcy said, smiling brightly.

"You're sure?" her mother asked.

"Sure I'm sure," Darcy said.

That evening she fixed up the dress as best she could—she took off the cap sleeves and added a patent-leather belt that matched her patent-leather flats, which still fit if she jammed her feet into them.

The next morning she got on the school bus

feeling hopeful. Perhaps her dress would even be considered trendy. But she knew it was going to be a nightmare after all when she saw the face of her new best friend, Suki Lamb, as soon as she got on the bus.

Darcy had met Suki the very first day they'd moved to Portland. Suki, who was very petite, was walking by Darcy's house with a dog bigger than herself. When the dog bounded away, Darcy caught him for Suki, and the two girls quickly became fast friends.

Suki had gotten into Kennedy, also. Although her family was poor, too, they weren't as poor as the Lakens. Suki had on a new miniskirt and a flowered T-shirt that looked just darling.

"What are you wearing?" Suki asked in horror as Darcy took a seat next to her.

"It's hip," Darcy said, swinging her hair over one shoulder. Suki didn't say anything else. Darcy sensed she didn't want to hurt her feelings.

The bus headed toward the wealthier neighborhoods, closer to the high school. Now other kids got on the bus, dressed in cool outfits that Darcy had seen in the display windows at the mall. They all seemed to know each other and they laughed and screamed at each other, standing in the aisles to talk, giving the bus driver the finger when he told them to sit down. It seemed to Darcy that some of the kids were looking at her and pointing and whispering, but she ignored them and talked with Suki all the way to school.

Just as Darcy was getting off the school bus, she heard a girl with blond curls whisper to another girl, "I'm not kidding! I saw that rag at the Salvation Army when I went in with my mother to make a donation." Both girls turned to look at Darcy. She held her head high and walked right by them.

Darcy found out quickly who the blond girl was—Marianne Reed, Miss Everything. And by noon, Marianne had told everyone just where Darcy had purchased her dress. Everyone was laughing, whispering, tittering behind Darcy's back. At lunchtime she took her sandwich outside to sit by herself in the sun. Suki was the only person she knew, but Suki had a different lunch period. Darcy closed her eyes and lifted her face to the sun, wishing she were anyplace else except in Portland, Maine, at Kennedy High School, wearing a brown dress from the Salvation Army.

"There she is," Darcy heard someone whisper. "Can you believe that dress?"

"She looks like the Jolly Brown Giant," another voice guffawed, and both of the girls cracked up.

"Well, what can you expect?" the first voice said. "She's just plain white trash."

Darcy opened her eyes. It was Marianne Reed, and she had just called Darcy white trash. Darcy had been raised to believe that a Laken always stood up for herself and her family. She'd also been taught to box by her older brother Sean.

Darcy stood up, wiped the crumbs off her fingers, and walked calmly over to Marianne.

Then she pulled back her fist and decked her.

It turned out that Darcy had broken Marianne's nose. She got called to Dr. Green's office and suspended on her very first day of school. Her mother was at work at the restaurant, so the principal talked to her father and told him that Darcy had been suspended. Sean came to pick Darcy up in the family's beat-up old Ford.

By the time Darcy left the principal's office, it seemed as if everyone at Kennedy

High knew what had happened. As Darcy walked down the hall to meet Sean, everyone was laughing and jeering at her. And she couldn't help herself—she began to cry. Sobs overtook her before she could make it out to the car. It was like feeding hungry sharks— her tears made the kids taunt her even more. Now they knew she was weak. Now they knew they could get to her.

And that was the first impression Darcy Frances Laken had made on her first day of high school.

That was then, this is now, Darcy reminded herself, giving herself a mental shake. She breathed deeply and willed back the tears that were threatening to overflow from her eyes. After all, she'd gone on to make some great friends at Kennedy. She'd been on the honor roll, been in two school plays, and excelled in the athletic department. And somewhere around her sophomore year, she'd grown into her looks and become comfortable with being tall and strapping. Some of the cutest guys in the school had started asking her out, and she'd dated fairly often. But still, somehow having Marianne, who didn't need the money at all, beat her out for the athletic scholarship—Marianne, who had remained her nemesis for all four years of high school—brought the old pain back as if it had happened yesterday.

The ceremony finally ended, and the seniors went running to their families for hugs and congratulations. Darcy made her way through the crowd to her own family and hugged her mother, then her father.

"I'm proud of you, girl," her dad said with his slight Irish brogue. Darcy's father, Connor, had come to the United States from Ireland with his family when he was six years old.

"Thanks, Daddy," Darcy said, grinning at him. She worried about him; she just couldn't help it. Ever since the stroke four years earlier, he'd grown increasingly frail. And for a man like Connor Laken, who had always prided himself on his strong body, it was a bitter pill to swallow.

"So you've gone and done it," Sean said, hugging his little sister. At twenty-four, Sean was the oldest. His bright blue eyes, red hair, and fair skin were in sharp contrast to his sister's looks. But then, Sean, Dean, and Patsi had inherited their father's Irish coloring, and Darcy, Patrick, and the baby, Lilly, had inherited their mother's dark coloring.

"Pick me up!" Lilly cried, pulling on Darcy's white graduation robe. Darcy picked up her three-year-old sister and swung her in the air.

Lilly was such a sweetheart—everyone in the family doted on her. Darcy suspected that Lilly was an accident, that before her, their parents had considered themselves done with having children. After all, Patrick was the next youngest, and he was already twelve. But the fact that her mother had conceived a baby after her father's stroke seemed to make Connor so happy—and now Lilly was the joy of the entire family.

"When are you going to graduate and earn your keep, huh, little one?" Connor asked the giggling Lilly.

"I didn't even start school yet!" Lilly protested, snuggling her face into Darcy's hair.

"Well, let's get it over and done with. Time's a-wasting!" her father chided playfully.

"Don't you listen to him, Lilly," Darcy told her sister fiercely. "One day you're going to go to college, and you're going to be someone very, very special!"

A lump formed in Darcy's throat all over again. If she could only manage to go to college in the fall, she would be the first one in the family to go beyond high school. But how was she ever going to afford it now?

"We'll figure something out," Shanna Laken said to her daughter softly, as if she had read Darcy's mind.

"You should have won the damned scholarship," twenty-year-old Dean said. "It wasn't fair."

"Don't curse, son," Connor said automatically.

Dean rolled his eyes. He worked in a shipyard, and heard things every day that would make your hair stand on end.

"Hey, Darcy!" Suki called, running over to her. "Come with me. I want my mom to get a picture of us together."

"Let me get one of you two before you run off," Shanna Laken said, lifting the family's inexpensive camera. Darcy put her arm around the diminutive Suki, who barely came to her shoulder, and they both smiled for the camera.

"Get one of all of us!" thirteen-year-old

Patsi suggested, and the whole family crowded in as Suki took their picture.

"I'll be right back," Darcy promised her family. She knew her mother had been scrimping and saving to take the whole family out to Riches—an inexpensive family-style restaurant—in honor of her graduation.

"Oh, please, look what crawled out from under its rock," Suki muttered when she and Darcy walked over to where her mother and brother were waiting. There was Marianne chatting with Suki's older brother, Andy. Andy had just finished his freshman year at the University of Maine, and Andy was, as Suki said, "a hunka-hunka-burnin' love"— or so all her friends told her. But then, Suki said that about Darcy's older brothers, too.

"I think it's incredible that you've already been published in *The Poison Pen!*" Marianne was gushing to Andy. *The Poison Pen* was the literary magazine at the University of Maine, and Andy had recently had one of his short stories printed there.

"God, she's disgusting," Suki whispered to Darcy. "She couldn't get him to ask her out last year when he was still at Kennedy, and he's not about to change his mind now that he's in college."

"Oh, hi, Suki, hi, Darcy," Marianne said perkily when Suki and Darcy walked over.

"Hi," Darcy said flatly, wishing that Marianne would simply go away.

"Too bad about the scholarship," Marianne told Darcy, shaking her curls away from her face. "I know you need that money *infinitely* more than I do."

"I'll get by," Darcy said coolly, staring Marianne in the eye.

"Good," Marianne said with a smile. "You know, confidentially, you're probably a better athlete than me."

"Garfield is a better athlete than you," Suki snapped.

"But the scholarship is about more than that," Marianne continued, ignoring Suki. "It has to do with character."

Darcy could feel the heat coming to her face. "Is that so?"

"It is," Marianne said earnestly. "And, well, no offense, Darcy, but the winner is supposed to represent Kennedy High. And you are not exactly what I would call representative of our community."

18

Darcy felt her fingers curl into a tight fist. She was itching, dying to pull back and punch that smug smile off Marianne's face. *You're not fourteen anymore and you can control your temper,* Darcy told herself, willing herself to unclench her fist. "You're entitled to your opinion," she managed to get out in a steely voice.

"No you're not," tiny Suki spat out, staring at Marianne. "Your opinions are as stupid and narrow-minded as you are."

Marianne grinned even more broadly, and Suki took a step toward her, but Darcy stopped her by putting a restraining hand on Suki's arm. "Forget it," she murmured.

"Temper, temper," Marianne chided. She laughed a tinkly laugh. "Well, I've got to run. 'Bye-bye now. 'Bye, Andy." She turned on her heel to head back to her large circle of friends and family.

And then the strangest thing happened.

It was as if a special light went on in Darcy's brain, as if her mind were an X-ray machine seeing things that no one else could see. For just a split second, instead of seeing Marianne, Darcy saw *into* Marianne, and then she saw Marianne's future.

She saw a tumor growing in Marianne's skull.

"Are you okay?" Suki asked Darcy.

"Wh-what?" Darcy asked. The flash was gone.

"You looked really weird there for a moment," Suki said.

"I'm fine," Darcy said.

But that wasn't true. Every once in a while, something similar happened. Sometimes things came to her in a dream, sometimes in this bizarre flash of light. But sometimes, somehow, Darcy just knew things.

When she was ten years old she'd had a flash in which she saw fire, just hours before their clothes dryer blew up in the basement, setting the lower part of their house ablaze. Another time she'd had a dream that her father was talking to her as if he were a baby. This had happened just two nights before his stroke, which had temporarily reduced his speech to garbled baby talk. Darcy had no control over the flashes, didn't know what they were or why she had them. The whole thing scared her so much that she usually tried to push it to the back of her mind.

But once again, Darcy just knew something. Marianne Elizabeth Reed had a deadly tumor growing in her brain, and Darcy Laken was the only one who knew it.

TWO

TWO

"I can't believe you're really leaving!" Darcy said, staring forlornly at Suki. They were in Darcy's bedroom (well, it was one-third hers, anyway—she had to share it with thirteen-year-old Patsi and three-year-old Lilly) just a week after graduation. Suki was moving to Los Angeles with her family, and she'd be going to U.C.L.A. in the fall.

"I can't believe it, either," Suki said. "I mean, I knew it was coming, but now that the day is finally here . . ." her sentence trailed off with a sigh.

Darcy knew just what Suki meant. They'd hashed out their plans for after graduation six months earlier. Suki's parents were divorced, and her father didn't help support the family at all. Her mother was a paralegal, and she'd gotten a good job in Los

23

Angeles. The only reason they hadn't already moved was so that Suki could finish high school with her class. She even had a summer job lined up in the same law office where her mother would be working. Since Suki was determined to become a lawyer herself, Darcy knew it was a wonderful opportunity.

As for Darcy, her summer plans were set, too. That very day she'd begin working at her uncle's ice cream parlor, Sweet Stuff, on the nearby resort island, Sunset Island. And since she didn't know how she'd ever be able to afford college in the fall, what would follow that was a great, big question mark.

"Listen, you're going to love it there," Darcy said firmly. "You're going to turn into a regular Valley girl!"

"Yeah, right," Suki laughed. "I've never heard of a Valley girl who was half-Chinese."

"So you'll start a trend." Darcy shrugged, smiling fondly at her best friend. *I'm going to miss her so much*, Darcy thought, feeling a terrible ache in her throat.

Suki looked at her watch and stood up reluctantly. "I guess I better go. My mom is frantically running around doing last-minute stuff—she's making me crazy."

"I have to go to work, anyway," Darcy said.

There was a moment of silence as the two friends stared at each other.

"God, I hate this," Darcy said, tears welling up in her eyes. "It really sucks."

"We'll write to each other," Suki promised, "and I'll come back and visit you as soon as I can." Suki threw her arms around Darcy and hugged her fiercely, tears streaming down her cheeks.

"Quit crying or you'll make me cry," Darcy said gruffly. She pulled back and looked at her petite friend, remembering how much they'd been through together, wondering if she'd ever really see her again.

"Catch ya later," Suki said softly.

"Later," Darcy echoed. It was what they always said to each other when Suki got off the school bus.

A tremulous smile, and then Suki was gone.

Darcy sat on her bed. She could hear the old clock on the table tick-tick-ticking. *Suki was here, now she's gone*, Darcy thought. *Everything changes. You can't hold on to anything.*

"Darcy, if you want a ride, get your butt down here!" Sean yelled up at Darcy.

"I'm coming!" Darcy yelled back downstairs. Sean was driving her over to Sunset Island for her first day of work. If she missed the ride, she'd have to take a bus, then a ferry to the island, and then the island trolley. She stood up, grabbed her purse, and took a last look at herself in the mirror. She'd followed all of her uncle's directions: She'd tied back her long hair, she was wearing the pink and black Sweet Stuff T-shirt he'd given her, and she'd donned a pair of black jeans. Darcy pushed some stray hairs off her forehead and made a face at her reflection. *You'll have to do*, she told herself, and bounded down the stairs.

As Sean drove toward the ferry to Sunset Island, Darcy stared out the window, lost in thought. The image of Marianne Reed came flashing into her mind. Now she was sorry she hadn't told Suki about her vision—that Marianne was terribly sick. Usually she told Suki everything. But somehow knowing that her friend was leaving forever made Darcy pull back, and so she hadn't told her.

Suki would have wanted me to tell her right away, Darcy said to herself. But then,

Suki was very dramatic, and Darcy was very pragmatic—in fact, Suki seemed a much more likely person to have "psychic flashes" than Darcy! She would feel like an idiot telling Marianne to check and see if she had a brain tumor. On the other hand, if she didn't tell and something was really wrong with Marianne, how was she ever going to forgive herself?

"Yo, Earth to Darcy!" Sean called.

"What?" Darcy said, startled. "Did you say something?"

"I could have told you the car was on fire and you wouldn't have heard me," Sean said. "I asked if you were going to talk to Uncle Pete about college."

Uncle Pete owned Sweet Stuff, and he was the only relative who had any money to speak of. Sean thought Darcy should hit Uncle Pete up for a loan for college.

"I can't do it, Sean, I really can't," Darcy said. Uncle Pete was Darcy's father's younger brother. He was forever telling Darcy and her brothers and sisters what a loser their father was. It made all of them crazy. On top of that, Darcy felt guilty that she hadn't contributed more to the family's dire financial situation. Oh sure, she'd always worked in the summers doing one thing or another, but during the school year her parents had insisted that she concentrate on her diving.

"That is just dumb—" Sean began.

"I can't stand the guy!" Darcy interrupted. "It's bad enough that I have to spend the summer working for him!"

"What's more important, your pride or going to college?" Sean demanded, staring hard at Darcy when he stopped at a red light.

"Dad would say my pride is more important," Darcy answered him, staring right back.

"Fine," Sean snapped, "spend your life working in an ice cream parlor, then."

Darcy didn't say anything. She knew Sean was just as frustrated as she was, that he felt guilty that he couldn't help Darcy go to college himself.

When the car pulled on to the ferry, Darcy got out and stared out at the vast ocean. The water reminded her of diving, and diving reminded her of the Belinda Kramer Award that she hadn't won. She wasn't in the best of moods when Sean pulled up in front of Sweet Stuff.

"Try not to tick Uncle Pete off too much, huh?" Sean said, putting his hand lightly on Darcy's arm.

"If he treats me fairly, I'll treat him fairly," Darcy said in a steady voice.

"Darcy, he's your boss," Sean reminded her.

"I doubt that's something Uncle Pete is going to let me forget," Darcy said. She kissed Sean lightly on the cheek and went into the ice cream parlor.

"Darcy, hi!" Uncle Pete said when he saw her. He looked at his watch and frowned. "You're five minutes late."

Darcy looked down at her own watch, which showed it was twelve o'clock on the dot, exactly the time she was supposed to be there. "I think I'm right on time," she said.

Uncle Pete frowned. The frown lines seemed to extend all the way back into his balding forehead. "Let's start off on the right foot, Darcy," he said. "When I said noon, I meant you start work at noon, not you arrive at noon. Got it?"

"Got it," Darcy echoed, biting back the retort she wanted to make.

Uncle Pete put his arm around her shoulder in a jocular fashion. "Hey, chin up!" he chided. "I'm just trying to instill a work ethic in my gorgeous niece, okay?"

Darcy moved out of his embrace. "My parents already taught me a work ethic," Darcy said in a stiff voice.

Uncle Pete threw his hands in the air. "You take everything the wrong way!"

"Sorry," Darcy mumbled. Maybe Uncle Pete was right. Maybe he really was just trying to be nice. *Yeah. And a barracuda is just a fish*, Darcy thought.

"Stow your purse behind the counter, and I'll show you around," Uncle Pete said.

He took Darcy on a tour, showed her where the huge vats of ice cream were stored, showed her the various types of cones and sundaes, and how the cash register worked. "Every day you cash out, and the register needs to tally up," Uncle Pete said. "If it's not right, it comes out of your check."

Darcy nodded. Although Uncle Pete was paying her six dollars an hour, which was significantly more than she'd been offered at other summer jobs, she couldn't afford to lose a penny of her income because of a stupid error.

"Today I'll be here for the whole afternoon," Uncle Pete said, "to make sure you got the hang of things. In a couple of days when the RKs get here, I'll add another girl on your shift."

"What's an RK?" Darcy asked.

"Rich kid," Uncle Pete laughed. "The island'll be swarming with them in about two, three more days. Maybe you'll meet a nice, rich guy! I bet Connor would love that, huh?"

"My father isn't interested in having me meet a rich guy," Darcy said, giving her uncle a look of disgust.

"Hey, Darcy, I was only kidding!" her uncle said heartily. "Lighten up, for pete's sake!" He shook his head and disappeared into his office, yelling back that she should call him if she needed him.

The bells on the front door rang as a mother and her young daughter came in.

"Hi," Darcy said. "Can I help you?"

"What kind of ice cream do you want, Melissa?" the woman asked the little girl.

"What kind do they have?" the little girl asked, twirling a brown curl around one finger.

"All the flavors are listed up here," Darcy said, indicating the large display board on the wall.

"I can't read yet," Melissa told Darcy solemnly. "You read them."

Darcy looked at the mother, who smiled benignly. Evidently she expected Darcy to appease her daughter and read off the twenty-five different flavors posted. "Vanilla, chocolate, strawberry, butter pecan—" Darcy began.

The bells on the door tinkled again and a group of five little boys wearing Little League outfits came in. They all started screaming at once and jumping around the shop. One boy had a water pistol. He ran after a little kid who cried and tried to run behind the counter.

"Whoa, no going behind the counter," Darcy said, catching the little boy as he tried to squirm away. "Don't you guys have an adult with you?" she asked.

"Coach is waiting in the van," a freckle-faced boy told Darcy. "I've got the bucks."

"Hey, you didn't finish reading the flavors to me!" Melissa whined.

"Get away from me, you snot-rag!" the little boy who had tried to run behind the counter yelled at the little boy with the squirt gun. He kicked the other kid in the shins. A bigger boy punched him hard in the arm and he started crying.

"Please ask your coach to come in here," Darcy told one of the boys who seemed reasonably quiet.

"He won't," the boy said pleasantly. "He hates us."

"Mommy!" Melissa whined even more loudly. "She isn't paying attention to me!"

Everyone was talking and yelling and crying at once. Darcy felt as if her head were rattling. She put two fingers in her mouth and whistled long and hard. Everyone in Darcy's family could whistle, but hers was the loudest in the entire Laken household. There was a moment of silence.

"Cool," a little boy said. "How did you do that?"

"If you form a line and order one at a time," Darcy began, "and if you put that squirt gun down, I'll show you."

"I'm first," Melissa screamed. "I'm first!"

"That's very, very good that you're asserting yourself, Melissa!" her mother approved.

"Would you please read the ice cream flavors to her while I wait on this group?" Darcy asked Melissa's mother.

"That isn't fair!" Melissa whined.

"That's true, darling," her mother agreed. "But let's talk about fairness. . . ." The mother took her daughter over to a table to chat. Darcy rolled her eyes and began waiting on the group of boys.

Finally all the boys had their ice creams, and the one with the money paid Darcy. While they licked at their cones, she showed them how to make a mouth-whistle extra loud—it had to do with an extra pucker on the sides of the lips. They ran out the door practicing their whistles.

"I let those boys go first," Melissa told Darcy.

"That was very nice of you," Darcy said.

"I want a vanilla ice cream cone," Melissa intoned.

"Isn't that cute? She always wants to know the flavors and she always has vanilla!" Melissa's mother laughed. "My daughter the purist!"

Darcy tried to return the woman's smile instead of telling her how badly she thought she was raising her obnoxious daughter. The woman waved good-bye and shepherded her darling little girl out of the ice cream store.

The next couple of hours passed quickly. Occasionally Uncle Pete stuck his head out to check on Darcy, but after the initial fiasco, things went smoothly. In the middle of the afternoon a group of four teenagers in riding regalia burst into the shop. Darcy stared at them wistfully, overcome with a sudden feeling of separateness. They looked so perfect with their expensive haircuts and jodhpurs and polished riding boots. Darcy pushed some stray hairs off her face and stood up a little taller. *You are who you are, and you're just as good as they are,* she told herself firmly.

"Well, of course you couldn't make the jump on that horse, Jenny!" a pretty girl with brown curls hooted to her friend. "Silver Fox is ancient! The little kids usually ride him!"

"Can I help it if my horse is pregnant?" the other girl asked. "Silver Fox was the only horse left to rent!"

"Can I help you?" Darcy asked the girls.

The girl with the brown curls smiled at Darcy. "Do you have crow-flavored ice cream for my friend, here? Because that's what she deserves to eat!"

"Just wait until Sugar foals," the other girl

replied, "and we'll have another jumping contest. Then we'll see who's eating crow!"

"You're on," the first girl promised. She smiled again at Darcy. "She hasn't got a chance," she said confidentially. She stared at Darcy contemplatively. "You look really familiar to me."

Darcy shrugged. "I just graduated from Kennedy in Portland."

"I go to Laudum, this hideous private school in Boston," Molly said, rolling her eyes. "It's supposed to be progressive—like for example, we don't get grades."

Darcy laughed. "Sounds good to me."

"Rowena goes to Kennedy," the girl said, pointing to a girl who was standing down at the other end of the counter. The girl looked up. Darcy hadn't noticed her when the group came in.

"Darcy!" Rowena called. "Hi!"

The brown-haired girl snapped her fingers. "Hey, now I know why you look familiar. You're on Rowena's diving team, right? I saw a picture of your team on Rowena's bulletin board!"

"Darcy wasn't *on* the team," Rowena said, "she *was* the team!" Rowena walked over to

Darcy. "We're going to be lost without you next year."

"Thanks," Darcy said with a small smile.

"And you got totally screwed on the scholarship, if you want my opinion," Rowena added.

Darcy shrugged. "Whatever."

"Hey, Molly!" one of the girl's called to the brown-haired girl. "They've got a new flavor called Monster Maple! They must have named it after your family!"

"Ha-ha," the girl said, definitely conveying that she didn't find the statement funny. She looked back at Darcy and thrust out her hand. "I'm Molly Mason," she said.

Darcy leaned over the counter and shook Molly's hand, impressed at the firmness of her grip. Darcy had a strong handshake—her father had taught her that. Most girls shook hands as if they were handing you a dead carp.

"So where are you going to college in the fall?" Rowena asked Darcy.

At that moment Uncle Pete came barreling out of his office. He stared pointedly at Darcy.

"Would you guys like to order?" Darcy asked dutifully.

"Jenny's buying, which means I'll have to indulge in a triple-dip of rocky road," Molly said, cocking her head toward the blond girl she'd been teasing. "She lost a major bet to me."

Darcy scooped out Molly's ice cream and all the rest of the group's ice cream orders under the scrutiny of her uncle. *Why does he have to pick this moment to watch over me like a hawk?* Darcy thought with irritation as she dipped a cone in nuts.

"Not like that!" Uncle Pete said, plucking the cone from Darcy's hand. "You got to hold it in the dip or the nuts don't stick!" He held the cone in the nuts as Darcy watched, feeling the heat coming to her face. "There you go!" Uncle Pete said with a wink, handing the cone to Jenny with a flourish. "Sweets for the sweet! How did all you gals get so pretty?"

God, he's nauseating, Darcy thought. *I'm so glad no one knows I'm actually related to him.*

"Oh, just your usual pact with the devil," Molly said breezily, licking at her ice cream cone.

"Ha! That's a good one!" Uncle Pete bellowed. "My niece here will finish taking care of you young ladies," he added, and walked back to his office.

Oh, thank you so much, Darcy thought with a wince. *Now the whole world knows we're related.*

Molly gave Darcy a sympathetic look. "Hey, don't sweat it. I have the weirdest parents in the world myself. You can't pick your relatives!"

Jenny paid for everyone's ice cream, and Darcy chatted with Rowena and Molly until more people came into the shop.

"Let's go," Jenny said. "I've got to get home and change before Johnny shows up."

"Johnny would love you even if you did smell like a horse," Molly said, laughing. She turned back to Darcy. "Hey, it was nice meeting you. Good luck with your diving." She smiled and walked out with her friends.

What a genuinely nice girl, Darcy thought, wiping the sticky ice cream off the counter. *She wasn't stuck-up or snobby at all. Nothing like Marianne Reed or her rich-bitch crowd.*

The fan blew some stray hairs into Darcy's face, and she impatiently pushed them away, not realizing that the back of her hand was covered with fudge topping and ice cream.

The fudge and ice cream tangled in the long strands of hair and made a gloppy mess that hung in her face. Annoyed, Darcy picked up the remains of a banana split which stuck to the counter for a moment, and then somehow spilled it on the front of her T-shirt. Before she could get back to the sink and clean off her hair or her T-shirt, the little bells tinkled at the front door.

Darcy looked up, gunky hair in her face and ice cream streaming down her T-shirt, into the smugly smiling face of Marianne Reed.

THREE

"Well, hi there!" Marianne said with surprise. "I didn't know you worked here."

"Now you do," Darcy said tersely, heading for the sink behind the counter.

"So I see," Marianne replied. She eyed Darcy with a bemused expression on her face, taking in the dripping T-shirt and gunky hair. "It looks like you're having a tough day."

"It's just ice cream," Darcy mumbled, wiping viciously at her T-shirt with a damp sponge.

"I hope you plan to wash your hands before you make my cone," Marianne said, making a face.

Darcy looked up at Marianne, ready to murder her. *Relax*, she told herself. *You don't have to kill her—nature is doing it for*

41

you. Instantly Darcy hated herself for having such a terrible thought. She felt as guilty as if she'd said it out loud—and even more convinced that she should tell Marianne about her psychic flash.

Darcy washed the gunk out of her hair, washed her hands, and asked Marianne what she wanted to order.

"Oh, blueberry ripple, I guess," Marianne said. "It's what I always get, but I never get tired of it."

Darcy made the cone and handed it to Marianne.

"I've been coming to Sweet Stuff forever," Marianne said chattily. She paid for her cone and licked it delicately. "We have a summer house here on the island."

"That's nice," Darcy said. Her mind was not on the conversation. She was trying to figure out just how to broach the subject of the inside of Marianne's head. . . .

"Of course, I always spent most of the summer at camp," Marianne continued, "but before my parents shipped me off, I'd get in a good two weeks on the island. It's the greatest place."

"Hmmmm," Darcy said noncommittally. She'd never spent any time on Sunset

Island—she thought of it as strictly the province of rich kids like Marianne. I mean, even an ice cream cone at Sweet Stuff cost three dollars!

There was only one tiny public beach, and it was over by the oldest and poorest section of the island. It was the worst part of the beach, too—so rocky on the bottom that you could cut your feet open just trying to go for a swim. The rest of the beachfront was privately owned. If the police came around and asked for ID when you were on the beach, you had to be able to prove you belonged there. Darcy had found that out the hard way when she was fifteen. She and Suki had gotten kicked off the beach—it had been totally humiliating.

"So . . . how are you feeling?" Darcy asked Marianne, seemingly out of the blue.

Marianne looked confused. "Oh, you mean about school being over and everything?" she finally said, figuring that's what Darcy was referring to. "I feel great! High school was terrific, of course, but college is going to be totally awesome. I'm going to be be twirling at Portland, you know," she added significantly.

"Sounds strenuous," Darcy commented. "I

guess you'll be getting a physical before you start college, huh?"

Marianne laughed. "Darcy, I've been twirling for five years; I think I can handle the strain."

"Maybe not," Darcy said carefully.

Marianne finished the last of her ice cream cone. "What are you talking about?" she asked, wiping some blueberry ripple off her pinky with a napkin.

Darcy stared hard at Marianne, willing herself to have another flash showing that horrible brain tumor. *If only I'd have a flash again, I'd know I was right to warn her,* Darcy thought desperately. But although she concentrated with all her might, all she saw when she looked at Marianne was blond curls and vacuous blue eyes.

Marianne stared back at her. "Darcy, you are acting very weird."

"Look, I know this is going to sound crazy," Darcy began, "but I think you should have a physical."

"You are not making any sense," Marianne said, "and I've got to go meet my friend Lorell at the Play Café, so—"

"Just listen to me for a minute," Darcy interrupted, "and then you can do whatever

44

you want." *Courage, girl,* she told herself. *Even if Marianne thinks you're a lunatic, you have to do this.* "Sometimes I . . . I get these feelings about things," Darcy began.

Marianne crossed her arms in front of her.

"For example," Darcy continued, "years ago I knew there was going to be a fire in our house before it happened."

"What did you do, set it?" Marianne asked dryly.

Darcy sighed. "Believe me, I know this sounds crazy, but I'm not losing my mind—I don't think," Darcy said in a rush. "At graduation I had this terrible premonition that you were sick."

Marianne raised her eyebrows and put her hands on her hips. "You don't actually expect me to believe that, do you?"

"It was as if I could see inside of you," Darcy said, ignoring Marianne's comment. "And I saw . . . I saw . . ." She faltered, not knowing how to tell Marianne the rest.

"Oh, do continue," Marianne said coolly. "I'm hanging on your every word."

"I saw a brain tumor," Darcy blurted out, "something wrong in your brain. . . ."

For a moment Marianne just stood there,

her jaw open. "You are the sick one here, Darcy Laken," she finally said.

"It's not that I want to scare you—" Darcy began.

"Bull!" Marianne exploded. "You're only telling me this because you're jealous you lost that scholarship to me."

"No, really, I—"

"Yes, really!" Marianne insisted. "Talk about a sore loser!"

"I knew this was how you'd take it!" Darcy yelled. "That's why I didn't want to tell you. I don't care what you think of me; just do yourself a favor and check it out."

Marianne gave Darcy a final look of total disgust, then she deliberately dropped her used napkin on the floor, turned on her heel, and walked out the door.

Well, I warned her, Darcy thought, as she came out from around the corner to pick up Marianne's dirty napkin. *That's all I can do.*

"How was your first day of work?" Darcy's mother asked her. It was around ten o'clock that evening, and Shanna had just gotten home from her waitressing shift at the restaurant. She kissed her daughter on the top of the head and put on the tea kettle, then sat down across from Darcy at the kitchen table.

"It was okay," Darcy said noncommittally.

"I know your uncle Pete isn't the easiest man in the world to get along with. . . ." Shanna began.

"That's the understatement of the year," Darcy murmured.

"He means well," Shanna said.

"So he keeps telling me," Darcy said dryly. "There's some meat loaf left from dinner, if you're hungry," she added.

"I ate at the restaurant," Shanna said, getting up to silence the tea kettle. "I worry about you, Darcy," she said softly. "This job and taking care of the little ones while I'm at work and all . . ."

"I'm okay, Mom," Darcy said. "Dad helps out when you're gone."

Shanna dunked her tea bag and gave Darcy a level look. "Believe me, Darcy, I know who does the work around here, and it isn't your father. I love him dearly, but he's an old-fashioned man—it hurts his pride to be home instead of out earning money for his family."

"Dad's fine just the way he is," Darcy said

tersely. She couldn't help it; she was unreasonably partial to her father. "Dad is—"

But the phone rang loudly before Darcy could finish her statement. She reached for it quickly, not wanting the ring to wake Lilly.

"Hello?"

"Hi, Darcy? It's Mark," came an easy male voice through the phone.

"Mark?" Darcy repeated, confused.

"Mark Greyson?" he said, laughter in his voice.

Mark Greyson! Mark Greyson had been just about the cutest guy in the senior class at Kennedy High. He was also a diver, and though he and Darcy had known each other for years, they weren't close friends, and he had certainly never called her before.

"Well, hi," Darcy said, the surprise showing in her voice.

"Hi. I hope I'm not calling too late," Mark said. "I called earlier, but I kept getting a busy signal."

"My little sister knocked the phone off the hook, and we didn't realize it," Darcy told him. Her mind was whirling. Mark Greyson was calling her! She pictured his shaggy blond hair and big blue eyes, and his swimmer's build that rippled with long, lean muscles.

"So, listen, some of the guys from the diving team are having a blowout tomorrow afternoon at McKinley's Park—we're planning a killer softball game. I thought you might like to go."

Darcy's heart sank. "I'd love to go, but I can't," she told him. "I'm working for my uncle in his ice cream parlor over on Sunset Island, and I have to work tomorrow."

"Hey, he's your uncle," Mark said. "He'll understand if you need a few hours off."

"No, he really wouldn't," Darcy said with a sigh.

"Can't you just ask him?" Mark said. "You do want to go, don't you?"

"Absolutely!" Darcy said quickly. How many times had she fantasized Mark Greyson calling and asking her out? Now it was actually happening, and she couldn't go! It wasn't fair! "Look, I'll call him and ask him," Darcy said. "How's that?"

"Cool!" Mark replied. He gave her his phone number. "So call me back and let me know."

Darcy hung up and turned to her mother. "That was Mark Greyson—one of the guys from the diving team. He invited me to a picnic tomorrow. He's really a nice guy. I really like him."

"Why is he calling you at ten o'clock at night for a picnic tomorrow?" Shanna asked, sipping at her tea. "It seems to me it's not very much notice."

Irritation flared inside Darcy, and she fought the feeling down. "It's not like it used to be," Darcy explained. "Kids don't plan things far in advance. It's much more casual. Anyway, he did try earlier, but the phone was off the hook." Darcy dialed her uncle's number and heard the phone ringing. She could feel her mother's eyes on her. *I don't care*, Darcy thought. *I'm allowed to not be perfect all the time.*

"Laken residence," came her cousin Alexander's voice through the phone.

"Hi, Alex, it's Darcy," she told him. "Is your dad there?"

"Dad!" Alexander screamed. "Darcy's on the phone."

"How's my newest employee?" Uncle Pete's voice boomed through the phone.

"I'm fine," Darcy said. She wrapped the phone cord around her hand nervously. "I was just wondering if I might be able to switch shifts with someone tomorrow."

"Why?" her uncle asked bluntly.

"Well, something came up that I'd like to do," Darcy began, "and I thought it might be possible to—"

"Darcy, Darcy, Darcy," Uncle Pete interrupted, "I'm very disappointed in you. You think this is professional behavior?"

"Well, no, but—"

"It shouldn't surprise me, coming from Connor's daughter, I suppose," her uncle continued. "I just didn't expect you to try to take advantage of me so soon."

Darcy's anger flared ominously. She longed to tell him just what he could do with his stupid job. But she forced herself to breathe more slowly, and willed herself to speak in a calm tone of voice. "Look, Uncle Pete, this has nothing to do with my father. And I'm not trying to get out of work—I just want to switch shifts. If the answer is no, just say so."

"The answer is no," Uncle Pete said. "And I'd like to point out that if I weren't your uncle, I doubt that you'd be asking for special privileges on your second day on the job."

"Maybe not," Darcy admitted.

"At least you own up to your mistakes," Uncle Pete said, "which is more than I can say for your father. I'll see you tomorrow, ready to work at twelve o'clock, right?"

"Right," Darcy agreed reluctantly.

"Good," her uncle said. "And, Darcy, someday you're going to thank me for teaching you how the real world works."

Darcy hung up and stared at the phone, as if she could will her poisonous thoughts through the wires to her odious uncle. With a sigh she picked up the phone again and called Mark back.

"Hello?"

"Hi, Mark," Darcy said. "I tried, but no luck."

"Well, that's a drag," Mark said. "It would have been fun."

"Yeah," Darcy agreed.

"So I'll call you another time," Mark promised before he said good-bye and hung up.

Shanna Laken sat watching her daughter. "Pete wouldn't give you time off, I take it."

"I really can't stand him, Mom," Darcy said.

"A job's a job," Shanna said. "It's your responsibility."

"I know that!" Darcy said irritably. "It's just . . . Oh, forget it. I'm going to bed."

As soon as Darcy walked out of the kitchen, she regretted being so snippy to her mother. None of this was Shanna's fault— her mother was doing the best she could. Her life wasn't easy, either.

But, oh, if only things could be different, Darcy thought as she brushed her teeth and washed her face. If only she could do what she wanted when she wanted. She'd go out with Mark, she'd spend her summer hanging out, working on her diving, being free. If only she could find a way to go to college in the fall, and not have to worry about every single penny.

Darcy undressed in the dark and slipped an oversize T-shirt over her head, then fell into bed. She could make out the shapes of her sisters, sound asleep. *I can't even have my own room and a little privacy,* Darcy thought miserably. *Sometimes I really hate my life.*

FOUR

It was a week later, and Darcy was just dashing out the door on the way to work—this time Sean had the car, and she was going to have to take the bus to the ferry—when the phone rang. She ran back into the kitchen to answer it.

"Hello?"

"Darcy?"

"Yes," Darcy answered. She didn't recognize the voice.

"It's Marianne."

"Oh, hi," Darcy said. Why was Marianne calling her?

"I just wanted to tell you that I actually went and had a physical," Marianne explained in a cool voice.

"I'm really glad you went," Darcy said quietly.

"Yeah, well, after I left the ice cream parlor last week, I was really upset," Marianne said. "Wouldn't you be if someone said something like that to you?"

"I guess so," Darcy agreed, "but I had to tell you."

"Oh, sure," Marianne snorted. "I'm sure you already knew the results of the physical."

"I'm so sorry," Darcy whispered.

"About what?" Marianne snapped. "I'm one hundred percent healthy."

"You're—?" Darcy began.

"You heard me," Marianne interrupted. "I'm completely and totally healthy—as if you didn't know."

"Are you sure?" Darcy asked.

"God, you are really pathetic!" Marianne yelled. "When I left the ice cream parlor, I figured you were just being bitchy, but I had the tiniest doubt that you were actually telling me the truth, that you had some weird psychic ability or something."

"I do!" Darcy exclaimed.

"Please," Marianne intoned. "I told my mother, and she was totally freaked out. I mean, my mother believes in this stuff—she actually has a private astrologer she consults every week. Her astrologer made me get the physical."

"But isn't it possible that—"

"That what?" Marianne shot back. "That the doctor missed my horrible brain tumor? God, why don't you just make a voodoo doll of me if you hate me so much!"

"I don't hate you—" Darcy said.

"I don't want to hear it," Marianne snapped, cutting Darcy off. "I just wanted you to know that I think you are total trash, and if I never have to look at your lying face again, it will be too soon."

"Marianne, I'm so sorry, I—" But Darcy heard the *click* of Marianne's receiver and the dial tone in her ear. She sat down in the nearest chair and stared into space.

How could this have happened? She had told Marianne she didn't hate her, but deep down inside, she knew she really *did* hate her, and she had ever since ninth grade. Had she really just imagined she saw a tumor in Marianne's brain because she had been so angry? Had it been some kind of awful, ugly wishful thinking?

Darcy caught a look at the time on the wall clock and bolted out of her seat. Even if she made great connections, she doubted that she'd get to Sweet Stuff on time. She grabbed her purse and ran out the door, feeling as if every awful thing that Marianne had said about her was true.

"Darcy! Pay attention, for pete's sake! That's the second time you scooped out the French vanilla when someone asked for regular vanilla!" Uncle Pete admonished her. "They don't get the high-test stuff unless they're paying for the high-test stuff."

"Sorry," Darcy mumbled. It was hard to concentrate on ice cream with her mind whirling around at a thousand miles per hour. How, how, how could she have imagined a tumor in Marianne's head? "I saw what I saw!" she insisted out loud, as she sponged the counter clean.

"What did you see?" Uncle Pete asked, looking up from some billing slips.

"Nothing—I'm talking to myself," Darcy told him.

Uncle Pete shook his head ruefully and headed into his office.

The store got busy for a while, not allowing Darcy any time to think about the awful mix-up with Marianne. Two hours later when there was a lull in business, Darcy poured herself a Coke and sat down to take a break. She was so lost in thought that she didn't even hear the bells at the door when someone entered the store.

"Looks like you're a million miles away," a friendly voice said.

Darcy looked up at a grinning Molly Mason wearing her usual riding regalia. Molly and her friends had been in for ice cream every day since Darcy had started the job, and Darcy and Molly had had a chance to talk a bit. Both were very independent, adventurous, and athletic. One big difference between them they had discovered, though—and it was really very funny—was that Darcy was afraid of horses, and Molly hated to swim!

"Hi!" Darcy said, smiling at Molly's friendly face. "I didn't even hear you come in." She looked around. "You're alone?"

"My friends all say they're gaining weight from our daily pig-out trips in here." Molly shrugged. "What can I say? I'm addicted to the stuff."

Darcy started to get up, and Molly stopped her. "I can wait," Molly said, sitting down opposite Darcy. "Enjoy your break."

"So how was riding today?" Darcy asked Molly.

"You ought to come with me sometime and try it," Molly said.

"Not me," Darcy laughed. "I can do a double gainer off the high board, but get me near a horse and I'm a total chicken."

"Did you have a bad experience with one or something?" Molly asked, shaking her brown curls out of her face.

"Not really," Darcy said. "I mean, no one in my neighborhood is in the income bracket to have an actual horse."

"Anyone can rent one, though," Molly said. She seemed completely unfazed by Darcy's reference to being poor which Darcy rather liked.

Darcy took a sip of her Coke. "My mom told me this story a long time ago," she mused, "about how a friend of hers got stepped on by her horse, and how one side of her face was permanently caved in. I had nightmares about it—this horrible caved-in face. . . ."

"Gruesome." Molly shuddered. "Okay, no horseback riding until further notice. How about parachuting from an airplane?"

"I've always wanted to try that!" Darcy exclaimed.

"Doesn't it sound awesome?" Molly asked. "So you'd really do it?"

"Absolutely!" she confirmed enthusiastically.

"I knew it!" Molly cried. "My parents have a friend who has a plane, and he teaches people to parachute. None of my other friends will go with me—"

"Aha!" Darcy laughed. "I'm the last resort!"

"You're the only person I know gutsy enough to do it!" Molly replied. "Even my boyfriend, Andy, won't try it."

"You didn't mention you had a boyfriend," Darcy said. She thought about Mark Greyson, whom she hadn't heard from since she had to turn him down for the picnic. So much for his promise to call again.

"Well, maybe that's overstating the situation," Molly admitted, brushing some lint off her jodhpurs. "His name is Andy Southerby, seriously cute, a car to die for, and he even has a brain. I've only been out with him three times, though."

"That's three more times than I've dated anyone lately," Darcy said ruefully.

"You?" Molly asked, wide-eyed. "You are

incredibly gorgeous! Guys must be dying to go out with you!"

"Thanks for the compliment," Darcy said, draining her Coke. "Actually, I don't meet all that many guys I really want to go out with, anyway." She got up and went behind the counter. "Pick your poison," she added, sweeping her hands across the array of ice cream vats.

"A double dip of chocolate-chocolate chip," Molly decided. She watched Darcy making the cone. "As far as I'm concerned, if it's not chocolate, it's not ice cream."

"A girl after my own heart," Darcy said, handing Molly the ice cream.

"Mmmmm, bliss," Molly sighed, after biting into the ice cream. "So when are we jumping out of an airplane?"

"You're serious?" Darcy asked.

"Absolutely," Molly confirmed. "And after that, we can try bungee-jumping!"

"That's where you jump off of a bridge or something and hang by your ankles from a bungee-cord, right?" Darcy questioned.

"You got it," Molly agreed. "Sounds great, huh?"

"I'm up for it." Darcy nodded. "That is, if I can afford it. My motto is—"

"I'll try anything once!" they both said at the same time, and then laughed together with delight.

"I can't believe it! You're so much like me!" Darcy exclaimed.

"On the inside, anyway," Molly agreed with a grin. "I'd love to be as tall as you are and have your incredible black hair. It's so long. Have you ever had it cut?"

"Just trimmed," Darcy replied.

"Guys must be crazed for it," Molly sighed, fingering her own chestnut brown curls.

"Hey, I'm the girl who hasn't had a date in weeks," Darcy reminded Molly.

"Your choice," Molly said with a shrug, crunching down the last of her ice cream cone. She reached into her purse and pulled out a small black card which she handed to Darcy.

"A business card?" Darcy said with surprise, reading Molly's name and address in raised red letters.

"My parents got them for my birthday," Molly said. "At the time I thought it was, like, the dumbest present anyone ever gave me. Now I think they're kind of cool."

"Different, anyway," Darcy said, slipping the card into the back pocket of her jeans.

"My parents have the same card," Molly said, "but theirs has a bloody thumbprint next to their names."

"A *what?*" Darcy asked.

"A bloody thumbprint," Molly replied breezily. "They write horror movies."

"That is so cool!" Darcy exclaimed. "Would I have seen any of them?"

"I hope not—they're really awful," Molly laughed. "We're not talking Stephen King here."

"I love horror movies; tell me some titles," Darcy urged.

"Oh, let's see, *Bloodsucking Cheerleaders, Revenge of the Mutant Mobile Phones, Death on a Platter—*"

"I saw that one!" Darcy screamed. "It was at the drive-in last year with *Return of the Nerds from Hell!*"

"Well, that's Mom and Dad," Molly said.

"That is so cool," Darcy repeated with admiration. "I never knew anyone in show business before."

"Yeah, well, my parents are not exactly what you'd call normal," Molly said ruefully. "You'll understand when you meet them. So call me and we'll arrange this airplane thing, okay? Maybe later this week?"

"Absolutely," Darcy promised.

Molly waved good-bye and headed out the door.

What a great girl, Darcy thought as she watched Molly leave. *I have a feeling we're going to become real friends.*

By the time Darcy had finished her shift and taken the trolley, ferry, and bus to get back home, her good mood from chatting with Molly had completely vanished. All the way home she ruminated about what had happened with Marianne. *The only good thing about the whole situation is that I'm not in high school anymore*, Darcy thought as she walked the last few blocks to her house. *If I were, Marianne would have spread it all over the school by now that I told her she had a brain tumor—it would be horrible.*

"Hey, baby, come over here and talk to me," a guy called to Darcy from outside the corner convenience store. Darcy ignored him and kept walking. Last week two girls had gotten beat up in front of that store by a gang of drunk guys.

For every law-abiding, friendly person living in the neighborhood, it seemed as if there were two lowlifes. As the economy got worse and more people were out of work, the neighborhood got scarier and the crime increased. Darcy turned the corner to her block and saw the large red letters painted on the street: Never Again, it read. It was there that a little girl jumping rope had been shot down, the innocent victim caught in the crossfire in a drug deal gone bad. The little girl had been just two years older than Lilly. *I'd kill anyone who hurt Lilly,* Darcy thought viciously, and hurried toward her house and her family.

"Hi, anyone home?" Darcy called when she walked in.

"Shhh," her father said, putting his finger to his lips. He pointed to the shabby living room couch where Lilly was sound asleep. "She fell asleep playing on the kitchen floor," he whispered, "and I moved her to the couch. That little one can fall asleep anywhere."

"You're not supposed to be lifting Lilly," Darcy scolded, kissing the bald spot on her father's head.

"I'll thank you not to be telling me what I should or shouldn't do, daughter," her father said as he limped over to the kitchen table and took a seat. "How was work?"

"It was okay," Darcy said. "It's not the world's most interesting job, if you want to know the truth." She got some lemonade out of the refrigerator and poured herself a glass.

"It's honest work," her father said.

Darcy sighed and drank her lemonade. That's what her parents always said—"It's honest work." As if that made the most boring job palatable!

"Anyway, it won't be for long," Connor said, patting his daughter's hand awkwardly. "You're much too smart to stay at such a job."

Darcy smiled at her father. He meant well, but how was she going to ever get a really good job if she couldn't find a way to go to college? The fact of the matter was that her diving scholarship was meaningful to her, but not worth very much financially. And the university had cut way back on financial aid possibilities in the last few years. It was just too depressing. Since she had no solution, she hated thinking about it.

Her mind turned again to what had happened with Marianne. Her father wasn't one to scoff at her psychic abilities—it was her mother who did that. Connor Laken was a man who believed in both hard, honest work and leprechauns.

"Dad, a very strange thing happened to me," Darcy began. She told her father the whole story about Marianne and the tumor. "So that's it," she concluded. "Now I feel like a complete idiot."

Her father stroked his chin for a moment. "And you say her physical exam showed nothing at all?" her father asked.

"Not a thing," Darcy said. "Could I have just imagined something wrong with her because I dislike her so much?"

"It seems doubtful," her father mused.

"Because if I could do that, I can never trust another psychic flash or dream of mine again!" Darcy exclaimed.

"Wouldn't it be possible," Connor began slowly, "that you were seeing into the future?"

"What do you mean?" Darcy asked.

"Well, what if nothing shows up on an X ray now because the sickness hasn't started to grow in her yet?" her father said.

Darcy's jaw dropped open. "You mean, she's healthy now but could get sick sometime later on? I was seeing something that just hasn't happened yet?"

"It's a possibility," Connor said gravely.

"That never even occurred to me," Darcy admitted. "It's also awfully hard for me to believe."

"Lots of things in this life are hard to believe, child," Connor said, "but that doesn't mean they're not true."

Darcy thought about this as she walked upstairs to her room. She had absolutely no idea what the truth was about Marianne. She didn't want to believe that she was a terrible enough person to fantasize a tumor in another person's head just because she disliked her, but on the other hand, the possibility that she was literally seeing into the future was too scary to even contemplate.

FIVE

Darcy was falling, falling through the air, held up only by the billowing parachute above her. She looked up at the blue sky, then down at the earth, and a sense of freedom and joy swept through her body. She looked over toward Molly, who had jumped right after her, but couldn't see her. Where was she? Darcy looked down, and it was as if her vision telescoped down, down, down to a road below her. As if it were the close-up in a film, Darcy saw the ambulance, the red flashing lights, a body being lifted out of a wrecked car. It was Molly! Oh God, it was—

Darcy sat up bolt-straight in bed, breathing hard in the darkness. What a terrible nightmare! She took huge gulps of air, willing her heartbeat to slow to a normal pace. *What is wrong with me?* Darcy thought, rubbing between her eyes. *I'm turning into some kind of ghoul, imagining terrible things!*

But what if it isn't just my imagination? a voice in her head persisted. *What if something awful is about to happen to Molly? This time you can't have imagined it out of wishful thinking, because you like Molly more than you've liked anyone except Suki. So what could it mean, then?*

"How about an overactive imagination?" Darcy mumbled out loud. She punched her pillow, turned over, and nestled back down into bed, willing herself to have happier dreams.

But when she woke up late the next morning, she felt anxious and tired, and the nightmare in all its details played over and over in her mind. She came downstairs and found her mother making eggs in the kitchen.

"Play with me, Darcy!" Lilly called, running over to her.

"Let your sister wake up," Shanna admonished her youngest child. She brought Darcy a glass of orange juice to the table. "Are you okay?" she asked, peering at her daughter. "You look tired."

"I didn't sleep very well," Darcy confessed. She drank down the orange juice and absentmindedly stroked Lilly's hair.

"Want to play Barbies?" Lilly asked hopefully, laying her head down on Darcy's lap. She had recently gotten two Barbie dolls from their church toy fund for needy children. They were Lilly's pride and joy.

"I have to go to work," Darcy said. Lilly's face fell. "How about when I get home later?"

"Later is a long time from now," Lilly said with a sigh, and trudged sorrowfully into the living room.

"That one should become an actress," Shanna said, setting a plate of eggs in front of Darcy.

"Mmmmm," Darcy said noncommittally. She wasn't really listening—she was thinking about her dream. Was it a psychic dream or wasn't it? How could she possibly tell? She reached into the back pocket of her jeans, and there was Molly's card. On impulse, she stood up and went to the phone, dialing Molly's number.

"Mason residence," came a very deep male voice.

"Is Molly in?" Darcy asked.

"Molly is not at home presently," the deep voice echoed in melodious tones. "Shall I take a message?"

"Tell her Darcy called," Darcy said. "I'll probably see her later this afternoon, anyway," she added, but left her number before she hung up.

Well, at least I tried to talk to her, Darcy thought as she ran upstairs to get ready for work. *Although if she had been home, I don't know what I would have said, anyway. "Don't drive your car"? "Be careful for the rest of your life"?*

Darcy was able to catch a ride with Sean, who was on the way to the gym to train for a boxing match that was coming up in two weeks. Darcy half listened as Sean went on about his latest opponent, a guy ranked much higher than he was.

"And if I win, I think George Cabretti will manage me," Sean was saying. "George is tops. I could go all the way with him behind me."

"That'd be great," Darcy said. She knew that Sean dreamed about making it as a boxer, just as she dreamed about . . . what? What were her dreams, exactly? Darcy sighed and stared out the window.

She knew she wanted wonderful things to happen to her, but she wasn't quite sure what she wanted those wonderful things to be.

"Have a good one," Sean called as Darcy darted into the ice cream shop.

Darcy walked in and stopped just inside the door. A slender, blond, pretty girl with a short, sexy hairstyle was behind the counter, dressed in the same pink and black Sweet Stuff T-shirt that Darcy was wearing.

"Hi," Darcy said, stowing her purse behind the counter.

"Hi," the girl said, sounding surprised. "Who are you?"

Oh God, Uncle Pete fired me and he didn't even tell me, Darcy thought miserably. "I work here. I think," Darcy added.

"Pete must have put on an extra girl earlier this summer," the girl said. She finished wiping the counter down and held out her hand to Darcy. "I'm Summer Bishop. I've worked here every summer for four years."

"Darcy Laken," Darcy said, shaking Summer's hand.

"Laken? As in Pete?" Summer asked.

"He's my uncle," Darcy confessed.

"Wow, are you lucky!" Summer squealed. "He's such a sweetheart!"

"Uncle Pete?" Darcy asked. "Are we talking about the same person?"

Summer laughed. "Oh, he just pretends to be an old meanie. I can joke him out of anything!"

"Great," Darcy said. This was really weird. The only jokes she'd ever heard Uncle Pete laugh at were his own.

"Hey, my two beauties are here!" Pete Laken called jovially as he entered the store. "Right on time, girls; that's what I like to see!"

"You know I'm always on time," Summer said, leaning over to kiss Pete's cheek. "Shame on you for not telling me about your niece!"

Pete blushed. "Show her the ropes, Summer," he mumbled, and scurried into his office.

"You got it!" Summer yelled to him.

"I already know the ropes," Darcy said. "I've been working here since last week."

"Well, I'll just supervise you to make sure," Summer said with a smile.

The bells at the front door jingled and a little girl and her mother walked in. It was

Melissa—the girl Darcy had waited on her very first day on the job.

"Can I help you?" Darcy asked politely.

"Read me the flavors, please," Melissa said imperiously.

"That's my girl!" Melissa's mother cheered. "You can assert yourself *and* say please, can't you?"

"The flavors are the same as they were last week," Darcy said sweetly. "You like vanilla, remember?"

"I want to hear the flavors," Melissa demanded, her eyes narrowing.

"Vanilla-chocolate-strawberry-butter-pecan-rocky-road . . ." Summer recited all the flavors in a flash. "And this week's special is praline chocolate chip!" she finished triumphantly.

"Wow, that was great!" Melissa said. "I'll have vanilla."

"Darcy," Summer said, cocking her head toward the vat of ice cream, as if Darcy were her employee.

What's her problem? Are her arms broken? Darcy thought as she dutifully scooped the ice cream out for Melissa.

"Thank you," said Melissa, taking the cone from Darcy. She looked Darcy over and licked her ice cream cone. "Your hair is pretty," she finally said, "but you're too big."

"That's an interesting observation, Melissa," her mother said, nodding as if Melissa had just suggested a solution to the crisis in the Middle East.

"That's a rude observation," Darcy told the little girl. "Besides, being big is good. It means I'm strong."

"Boys don't like it, right?" Melissa asked, looking to Summer for confirmation.

"Right!" the petite Summer confirmed with a wink.

"Now, Melissa, we don't define ourselves by what boys think, do we?" Melissa's mother coached.

Melissa just shrugged and licked away at her ice cream. Her mother handed the money to Darcy and smiled. "So much for my budding feminist," she said, and ushered her little darling out of the store.

"That child is a good argument for zero population growth," Darcy said, ringing up the sale.

"I thought she was cute," Summer said, leaning against the counter.

"She might have been, if her mother hadn't ruined her," Darcy said. Her own parents

were the exact opposite of Melissa's overin-
dulgent mother.

A woman who looked like an older version
of Summer breezed into the store, carrying
an armload of shopping bags.

"Hi, honey," the woman said, walking over
to kiss Summer on the cheek. "I just blew a
fortune down at the boutiques."

"What did you get for me?" Summer
asked.

"All the stuff for me that you'll borrow and
never return," the older woman said with a
laugh. She put down her bags and turned to
smile at Darcy. "Hi, I'm Nancy Bishop,
Summer's mom."

"Darcy Laken," Darcy said, introducing
herself.

Nancy's eyes widened. "You're Pete's
niece?" she asked.

"Right," Darcy confirmed. Evidently this
woman knew her uncle.

"He never told me his niece would be
here," she said. She looked at her daughter,
but Summer just shrugged. "Is he in the
office?"

"Doing the books," Summer told her
mother.

"Excuse me," Nancy Bishop said, and walked into Pete's office.

Something very strange is going on here, Darcy thought with trepidation. "Is your mom a friend of my uncle's?" she asked Summer.

Summer busied herself by examining a hangnail in detail. "Something like that," she finally said.

"What does 'something like that' mean, exactly?" Darcy asked.

Summer looked up. "He's your uncle," she said. "Ask him yourself."

Okay, it's none of my business, Darcy told herself. *If Uncle Pete is having an affair with this woman, it's his business. Maybe it's not even what I think it is, anyway.* But a nagging voice told her it was exactly what she thought it was, and she couldn't help feeling shocked. After all, he was married and had a large family.

Nancy walked out of Pete's office, then turned around and blew a kiss in to him. It seemed to Darcy that Nancy was going out of her way to make sure that Darcy witnessed this. She gave Darcy a defiant look, whispered something to her daughter, and walked out of the store.

Two customers came in and Darcy waited on them while Summer stowed her mother's packages behind the counter. Finally the store was empty again, and Uncle Pete came out of his office.

"I'm going for lunch," he told them, not making eye contact with Darcy.

"Mom said you were going to meet her at The Fisherman's Wharf," Summer said, naming an excellent seafood restaurant on the island.

"Uh, yeah," Pete said, blushing furiously. "Hold down the fort, girls," he added, and hurried out the door.

"Is something going on between my uncle and your mother?" Darcy asked bluntly.

"Like I said, ask him yourself," Summer said, folding her arms defensively.

"Why do I have the feeling that it's something my aunt Jeanette—Uncle Pete's *wife*—" she emphasized the word "wife" for Summer's benefit "—doesn't know about?"

"If she hasn't known for the past five years, I see no reason to tell her now," Summer said coolly.

Five years! Uncle Pete had been having an affair with this woman for five years? Darcy couldn't even imagine her uncle having sex at all, much less carrying on some long-term torrid relationship!

Some customers came in, and even when it got busy, Summer did no more than "supervise" while Darcy did all the work.

"You missed a spot," Summer said, pointing to a spot of hot fudge left on the counter.

Darcy whipped around. "What is it with you? I thought we were *both* supposed to be working."

"I'm supposed to be showing you the ropes," Summer said defiantly.

"All you're doing is sitting on your butt!" Darcy yelled.

"You're just pissed because your uncle is in love with my mother," Summer yelled back. "He's going to marry her, you know."

"He's got six little kids at home!" Darcy protested. "Don't you think that's kind of messed up?"

"Pete will still support them," Summer shot back. "He's helped support us for years!"

Darcy's jaw fell open. Her uncle was supporting another family? No wonder Summer thought he was such a terrific guy!

"He's really great," Summer said earnestly, as if she could read Darcy's mind.

"He's even paying part of my college tuition in the fall!"

Unbelievable. Here she was, his niece, unable to ask for his financial help so she could go to college, and he was sending his girlfriend's daughter like it was nothing. Life was just so weird.

The store got busy again and Darcy worked hard. She kept hoping that Molly would come in. She really needed someone to talk to, and somehow she felt as if she could confide in Molly. Sure, she could call Suki in California, but it would help to be able to talk to someone who was around.

Uncle Pete and Nancy Bishop came back a couple of hours later. Darcy saw them holding hands as they walked up to the door, then saw her uncle deliberately drop Nancy's hand as they came inside.

"We had a great lunch!" Nancy told her daughter gaily.

Darcy looked pointedly at her uncle, but he scurried into his office. Nancy picked up her packages and turned to Darcy. "It was nice meeting you," Nancy said.

"Thanks," Darcy said. "Would you like to meet my cousins, too—Pete's six kids?"

Nancy flushed and lifted her chin defiantly. "I'm quite aware of their existence," she said smoothly.

"Funny," Darcy said, "they're not aware of yours."

Nancy's lower lip trembled and she took a deep breath. "Look, I've hidden this relationship for years, and as I just told Pete, I don't intend to hide it any longer! I will not live that way anymore! I'm glad you found out!"

"Actually, you sort of shoved it in my face," Darcy replied in a steely voice.

To that, Nancy Bishop had no response. She turned and marched out of the store.

By the time Darcy was doing her final cleanup, Molly still hadn't shown up. Darcy was disappointed—this was the very first day since she'd started working that Molly hadn't come in after her riding lesson for ice cream. Darcy's dream flashed in her head again—the ambulance, the car crash, Molly on a stretcher. Could that be why Molly hadn't come in? Darcy shivered. *You are really letting your imagination run away with you,* she told herself as she wiped down the glass in front of the ice cream vats.

"See you tomorrow," Summer called as she picked up her purse and headed for the door. The final prep work was only half-done, and thus far Darcy had done it all while Summer read a magazine.

"I hope you're planning to share the work tomorrow," Darcy told her.

Summer didn't answer—she just rolled her eyes and walked away. Darcy was infuriated. If the same thing happened the next day, she vowed she'd speak with her uncle about it.

Yeah, and how much good do you think that's going to do? she asked herself as she lugged the heavy buckets of ice cream up from the storage room. *He's sleeping with her mother. He's sending her to college. He's not going to stick up for you, the daughter of the brother he's never gotten along with.*

By the time Sean came to pick her up, Darcy was really ticked off. She was in a no-win situation and she knew it. On top of that, the option of ever asking Uncle Pete for a college loan now seemed totally hopeless. No way was he going to pay to send both her and Summer to college simultaneously. *I suppose I could blackmail him, Darcy mused, threaten to tell Aunt Jeanette about his little playmate.* But Darcy knew she would never, ever do that. It went against the way she'd been brought up, and besides, it just wasn't her style.

After dinner, Darcy ran up to her room to get Suki's new phone number. The more she thought about the situation with her uncle, the angrier she got. She just had to talk with someone!

She waited impatiently for Patrick, then Sean, then her mother, to finish using the phone, then she picked it up quickly before anyone else got to it. She dialed Suki's new number, but there was no answer.

Would it be too presumptuous to call Molly Mason and confide in her? But Molly was such a new friend, it might be awkward talking about such personal family stuff.

"Oh, what the hell," Darcy said out loud, and dialed the number on the black business card.

"Mason residence," came the deep, melodious voice.

"Hi, is Molly home?" Darcy asked.

There was a beat of silence.

"Who's calling, please?" the voice asked.

"This is a friend of hers, Darcy Laken."

"I'm afraid Molly has been in an accident," the voice said.

Darcy could hardly breathe. "A car accident?" she whispered.

"Yes," the voice said. "She's at Memorial Hospital."

"Is she . . . ?" Darcy couldn't even finish her question.

"She's in critical condition," the voice said.

Darcy mumbled something and hung up. She was stunned, unable to move.

"Honey? Are you okay?" Shanna asked as she walked by.

"My . . . my new friend on Sunset Island was in a car accident," she managed to gulp out.

"Oh, that's terrible!" Shanna cried, reaching for her daughter. "Is she okay?"

"She's in critical condition at Memorial Hospital," Darcy said. "I've got to go. Can I take the car?"

"Yes, of course," her mother said. "She's probably not allowed to have visitors yet, honey," she added gently.

"It doesn't matter," Darcy said. "I've got to go." She grabbed the car keys and her purse, and ran for the car.

My fault, my fault, my fault, a hideous voice in Darcy's head echoed as she headed for the hospital. *I got so caught up in worrying about work and my stupid uncle that I didn't warn Molly. I could have, but I didn't. Whatever happens, it's all my fault.*

SIX

"You've got to stop blaming yourself, daughter," Darcy's father told her, gently stroking her hair.

It was more than a week later, a rainy Saturday morning, and Darcy and her father were alone in the kitchen. Three days earlier, Molly had finally gotten out of intensive care. Although she hadn't been allowed any visitors except her parents, whenever Darcy wasn't working, she kept a vigil at the hospital. The dark circles under her eyes attested to her exhaustion, and both her parents were worried about her health. Only her father, however, knew why Darcy felt so responsible for her friend.

"How can I not blame myself?" Darcy responded, rubbing her eyes wearily. She got up to put on a fresh pot of coffee.

"The good Lord works in mysterious ways," Darcy's father said. "Perhaps this was just His will."

"Then why did I have the dream, Dad?" Darcy asked, measuring the coffee into the filter. "I just don't believe God wanted Molly hurt in a car accident."

"These things are not for us to understand. . . ." her father began.

"I can't swallow that, Dad!" Darcy exclaimed, whirling around to face her father. "I believe we have free will. And I also believe in logic. Logically I knew about Molly's accident and didn't warn her, so I'm at fault!"

"And maybe there're lessons the both of you were meant to learn from this, because of a greater plan," Connor Laken said softly. "Maybe you should talk it over with Father Perry."

"Father Perry hasn't got any answers for me," Darcy said sadly. "No one has any answers." She flipped on the switch to the coffee maker and headed to her room to get dressed to go to the hospital. Today was the first day Darcy would be allowed in to see Molly. What no one knew, not even Darcy's father, was how much Darcy was dreading it. Because Darcy knew what the doctor would be telling Molly today, something he'd told Molly's parents the day before when Darcy had been there, sitting with them in the lounge. Molly's back had been broken—a lumbar vertebra was fractured. The doctors said she was never going to walk again.

Darcy took a deep breath, and then pushed open the door to Molly's room. She was by herself, in a room filled with flowers and get-well cards. Her red-rimmed eyes looked bleak and hopeless. And Darcy knew that she knew.

"Hi," Darcy said, just inside the door. "Feel like company?"

"Not really," Molly answered.

"Should I go away?"

"I don't care," Molly answered in a voice filled with misery.

Darcy hesitated. "I could come back later. . . ."

"No, come on in," Molly said. "I don't know what I want."

Darcy pulled a chair up to Molly's bed. "Great flowers," she said, looking around at the blossoms.

"It smells like a funeral parlor in here," Molly said. "I wish it *was* a funeral parlor."

Darcy remained silent. Some inner voice told her not to give Molly any platitudes about a positive attitude just at this moment.

"My parents told me you've been here every day," Molly said, changing the subject abruptly.

"I was worried about you," Darcy said quietly.

"I guess Andy wasn't," Molly said, giving a short, sardonic laugh. "He hasn't been here at all. Oh, he did send flowers—that huge, ugly arrangement by the window."

"Some people just hate hospitals," Darcy said.

"Yeah, me," Molly replied. She looked out her half-open door and Darcy saw her watch an old woman in a tattered robe making her way painfully down the hall, a younger woman helping her. Molly's eyes filled with tears. "I can't feel my legs anymore," she sobbed. "This morning the doctor told me I'm never going to walk again."

"Oh, Molly," Darcy cried, feeling her friend's despondency. She put her hand on Molly's arm, but Molly seemed transfixed by the old woman in the hall who was slowly moving out of view.

"It can't really be true, can it?" Molly asked Darcy, her eyes overflowing with tears. "I'm only sixteen years old!"

There was nothing that Darcy could say, so she just held Molly's hand and let her cry.

"I remember I saw this movie on TV once," Molly said finally, blowing her nose. *"The Other Side of the Mountain*. It was about a girl, some famous skier, and she was paralyzed in a skiing accident. She was determined she'd walk again, and she fought and fought."

"And did she?" Darcy asked.

"No," Molly said. "And she was a hell of a lot braver than I am."

"Knock-knock!" came a voice from the door. Darcy and Molly turned to see Rowena and Jenny, Molly's two riding buddies. Rowena was carrying a huge teddy bear dressed in full riding regalia. He even had his own riding crop stuck in his paw.

"Wow, you look so much better!" Rowena cried, kissing Molly's cheek and setting the bear down on the windowsill.

"Better than when?" Molly asked. "This is the first day I've seen you guys."

"We've been here three times," Jenny said, "but the nurse wouldn't let us in to see you." She turned to give Darcy a smile of hello.

"We peeked in anyway, though," Rowena said. "You were sleeping."

"I don't suppose Andy has been here at all," Molly asked her friends.

"Maybe he came when you were asleep," Jenny suggested.

"Maybe he didn't come at all," Molly said bleakly.

"So listen, when do you get to blow this place?" Rowena asked. "Ebony misses you."

Molly and Darcy exchanged a quick look. Evidently Molly's friends didn't know her legs were paralyzed.

"Pill time," a nurse called, bustling into the room. She handed Molly two pills and gave her a small cup of water to wash them down. "I'm sorry. One of you will have to leave," she told the girls. "Only two visitors are allowed in here at a time."

"I'll just go for a walk and let the three of you talk," Darcy said, getting up quickly. She walked down to the cafeteria for a cup of coffee, and saw Molly's parents sitting by themselves at a table in the corner.

"Hi," Darcy said softly, sitting down next to Molly's mother.

"Hi," Molly's mother responded with a tired smile. "Were you just in with her?"

Darcy nodded. "Two of her riding friends just came in, so I left for a while."

"You're a really good friend to her," Molly's dad told Darcy. "It's amazing that the two of you have known each other such a short time." Darcy had told Molly's parents how and when she and Molly had met.

"Well, sometimes you just click with someone, I guess," Darcy said, staring guiltily into her black coffee. *Would I spend so much time here if I didn't feel so guilty?* Darcy wondered. It was a question to which she didn't have an answer.

"Have the police had any luck tracking down the person who hit Molly?" Darcy asked, wanting to change the subject.

During the many hours that Darcy had spent at the hospital with Molly's parents, they'd told her everything they knew about the accident. Molly had been driving on Shoreline Road, coming around the bend toward the island's main shopping area. It appeared that a car coming around the blind curve had overshot the bend and hit her car on the passenger's side. The force of the impact had sent Molly's car into a tree on the driver's side. At least that's what the police surmised had happened. The accident was a hit and run, and there were no witnesses. In fact, so far, Molly had no memory of the accident at all.

"No, nothing," Molly's father said with disgust. "What kind of a person would do that and just drive away?"

"A very scared person," Molly's mother said.

"That's too noble for me," Molly's dad replied, his hand clenching and unclenching into a fist. "I want the person found and fried."

"Frying only happens in our movies, dear," Molly's mother said, trying for some gentle humor. But Mr. Mason wasn't interested in any kind of humor. His eyes remained dark and stormy.

Through the glass wall of the cafeteria Darcy saw Rowena and Jenny walking by. She waved and they came in.

"Hi, girls," Mrs. Mason said, smiling wanly at her daughter's friends.

"Hi," Rowena said. "Molly looks a lot better."

"Yeah," Jenny agreed. "She told us she's getting out soon, that all she needs is some kind of physical therapy stuff that she can come in for every day!"

"That's what she said?" Mrs. Mason asked carefully. "Some kind of physical therapy?"

Rowena nodded. "For her broken legs, I guess."

Darcy stared down at the table. So Molly hadn't told her friends that her legs were paralyzed.

"They do have a therapy program here that she can do as an outpatient," Mr. Mason agreed, "once she's done the first two weeks here."

"Great," Jenny said. "She'll be back on Ebony in a couple of months, I bet."

Rowena laughed. "Knowing Molly, she'll be jumping out of planes by then!" The two girls said their good-byes and hurried off.

"She didn't tell them," Mr. Mason said in a flat voice.

"We should go talk to her, Gomez," Molly's mother said, getting up from her chair.

"And say what?" Mr. Mason shot back. "'Dear, maybe you should mention to your friends that you're never going to walk again, much less ride your horse'?"

Mrs. Mason turned to Darcy. "You go in," she urged Darcy. "She knows you know the truth, right?"

"Yes," Darcy agreed.

"I think our sadness is a terrible burden to her," Molly's mother said intensely. "It might be easier for her to discuss it with you."

Darcy nodded, drained her coffee, and headed back to Molly's room. Molly's eyes were closed, and Darcy had started to tiptoe back out when Molly called to her.

"Come on in, I'm not sleeping," Molly called. "I'm just trying to pretend I'm not here."

Darcy came and sat by Molly's bed. "Did you have a good visit with your friends?"

"Sure," Molly said in a flat voice.

"I saw them in the cafeteria before they left," Darcy told her.

Molly looked at her. "So you know I didn't tell them."

Darcy nodded.

Molly flung one hand over her forehead. "I couldn't. They wouldn't understand."

"They'll find out eventually," Darcy said practically.

Molly turned to stare at her. "And then what?"

"Well, I think—" Darcy began.

"I'll tell you what," Molly interrupted. "They'll pity me. They'll talk to me in whispers, and tell me how everything is going to be okay. Then behind my back they'll call each other on the phone. 'Can you believe what happened to Molly?' they'll say to each other. And they'll feel so lucky and superior, because nothing bad is ever going to happen to them."

"Bad stuff happens to everyone," Darcy said quietly.

"But it doesn't get all evened out, does it?" Molly snapped. "More bad stuff happens to some people than to others, and no one knows why."

"That's true," Darcy said. "I think about that sometimes."

"I never thought anything bad would happen to me, either," Molly said. She smiled bitterly. "You know what my friends call me? Maniac Mason, because I was never afraid to try anything." She stared hard at Darcy. "And don't try to tell me that now I'm afraid to try and get better, or I'll just scream."

"Got ya," Darcy promised.

"I just keep thinking—*why me?*" Molly

said in a hushed voice. "Am I being punished?"

"I don't believe that," Darcy said firmly. "It's just . . . random. Just horrible and random."

Molly stared past the teddy bear on the windowsill out at the beautiful clear blue sky. "In that case, the world sucks," she said, "and I can't think of any reason to even be alive."

Every response Darcy could think of sounded banal and empty, so she just reached for Molly's hand, and didn't say anything at all.

SEVEN

"I loathe physical therapy," Molly said bluntly, and pulled the covers over her head.

"Too bad," Darcy said, and pulled the covers back down. "I promised I'd get you into the physical therapy room by ten o'clock, and that's what I'm going to do."

Molly peered at Darcy through narrowed eyes. "When did you turn into such a hard-ass?"

"It's just my natural charm," Darcy said, lifting Molly into her wheelchair.

It was ten days later, and Molly had fought the physical therapy process every step of the way. It was ironic, really, because other than her spinal cord injury, Molly hadn't been that badly hurt. The doctors felt that she could be making much more rapid progress in her rehabilitation, if only she had the desire to do so.

Darcy had been spending every morning at the hospital. The Masons had very kindly arranged for a private car to take her to work at Sweet Stuff after her visits. For some reason, Darcy seemed to be the only person whom Molly would really talk to. She shut out her old friends—who finally all knew the truth about her injury—and even seemed uncomfortable around her parents. But somehow with Darcy, with whom she had no history, she could be herself. Darcy didn't coddle her, or pity her, and she wasn't cowed by Molly's anger. She was also the only one who could easily lift Molly into her wheelchair.

"These exercises are pointless," Molly groused as Darcy wheeled her down to the physical therapy room.

"No they're not and you know it," Darcy said. She took the wheelchair around the corner at a quick pace.

"Enter me in the Indy Five Hundred, why don't you?" Molly complained, but she smiled in spite of herself.

"Hi, Molly, how are we feeling today?"

asked Pixie Lawless, the perky therapist who supervised Molly's therapy.

"*We* are feeling like crap," Molly snapped. She had asked Pixie to please not use "we," as if she and Molly were the same person, but Pixie had just laughed her tinkly laugh and kept right on doing it.

"We're going to start with upper-body strengthening exercises today!" Pixie chirped, handing Molly a weighted ball. "Shall we do this to music?"

"Shall we just shut up?" Molly asked Pixie.

"Now, now, we're not cooperating!" Pixie *tsk*ed.

"Look, I'll make you a deal," Molly said between clenched teeth. "You stop using the royal *we*—which is unbelievably obnoxious—and I'll do my exercises like a good little girl."

"Well, gee, okay!" Pixie agreed. "How about some music? Just to get you into the spirit of it. What do you like?"

"Gregorian chants," Molly muttered.

Pixie rummaged through her cassettes. "How about an oldie but a goodie?" She pushed a cassette into her portable tape player, and the sounds of the Supremes singing "Stop! In the Name of Love" filled the air. "And one-two, one-two!" Pixie called out, bending Molly's arm in time to the music.

"This is dumb! This is stupid!" Molly chanted in rhythm.

"Really good!" Pixie cheered when she'd finished Molly's series of upper-body exercises. "Now we'll move on to the bars."

This was the part that Molly hated the most. Wearing heavy leg braces, she was learning to stand and then "walk" between two metal bars by pulling her dead legs along with the strength of her arms.

"Shall we have music for this one, too, Molly?" Pixie chirped enthusiastically. "What do you like?"

"Silence is a workable option," Molly suggested dryly.

Pixie giggled. "You have the greatest sense of humor," she said, bending down to fit Molly's braces onto her legs. "Oops! I've got to run to the little girls' room," she realized, straightening up. "Back in a jiffy!"

"God, I can't stand her," Molly groaned when Pixie had pranced out of the physical therapy room.

"She is nauseating," Darcy agreed, reaching down to fit Molly's right leg into the brace. She'd helped Pixie do it so many times that now she knew the whole procedure.

"How about if I just strangle her with my massive upper-body strength?" Molly asked.

"It might be a service to humanity," Darcy agreed with a laugh, checking Molly's brace carefully.

"Can you imagine some guy marrying her?" Molly asked. She screwed her face up in an accurate imitation of Pixie's cutesy mannerisms. "Gosh, honey-buns, are we going to have sexi-poo tonight?" she asked, mimicking Pixie's voice to perfection.

Darcy laughed. "That was very good."

"I have hidden talents," Molly replied. "Maybe I could get together with the other crips and start a mutiny. We could call ourselves Lumps Against Lawless."

"Does it make you feel better to call yourself names like 'crip' and 'lump'?" Darcy asked.

"Yeah, as a matter of fact, it does," Molly answered. "And please do not lecture me about having a positive attitude, or I will just scream."

"No lecture," Darcy promised, "but you aren't exactly pleasant to be around." Darcy reached for the other brace and fitted it on Molly's left leg.

"Well, excuse me, being pleasant isn't high on my agenda right now," Molly snapped.

"I can understand that," Darcy said, "but it's hard on your parents and your friends."

Molly shrugged sullenly.

"Rowena called twice yesterday while you were in the whirlpool," Darcy told Molly, checking the fit of the left leg brace.

"You already told me that," Molly seethed.

"So call her back, then," Darcy said. "She just wants to know when she can come visit."

"Don't you think I know it's all a crock?" Molly asked. "I mean, when any of my so-called friends come to visit, they find an excuse to leave five minutes after they arrive!"

"That's because they're uncomfortable, and because you treat them like dog meat," Darcy answered honestly.

"Yeah, well, I treat you like dog meat, too," Molly said, studying Darcy, "and you stick around. Now, why is that?"

Darcy looked away, afraid for Molly to look into her eyes. *If she knew the truth about me, she'd hate me forever*, Darcy thought. And yet she knew that it was more than guilt that compelled her to spend so much time with Molly, foul temper and all. She struggled to try and express how she felt.

"I guess I think that if what happened to you had happened to me, I'd be at least as angry as you are," Darcy began slowly. "I know what it feels like to be so angry that I want to just lash out at the nearest target—I haven't always been so wonderful at controlling my temper," Darcy admitted ruefully.

"Join the club," Molly said with a sigh.

"When you say mean things, I just think—*yeah, right, she's pissed off, and rightly so,*" Darcy continued. "I can't possibly know how you feel; it would be stupid for me to pretend that I do. I figure you've got to find your own path through this, work it out your own way."

"You're the only one who seems to understand," Molly whispered, her eyes filling with tears. "With my parents, I feel like I have to be all sunny so that they won't feel so bad. And with my other friends, I just can't stand how they look at me now. I don't know if I'll ever be able to stand it." Molly looked up at Darcy. "But it's different with you. I can talk to you."

"I'm glad," Darcy said simply.

"Okeydokey!" Pixie cried as she flew across the physical therapy room. "Time to rock and roll! Did you pick out some terrific music?"

"No," said Molly.

"Ah, here's a goodie!" Pixie squealed, pulling a cassette out of her pile. She popped in the cassette, and Madonna singing "Like a Virgin" filled the room.

"That's so inspirational!" Molly cried sarcastically. "Now that I'm going to spend my entire life as a virgin and everything."

"Upsy-daisy!" Pixie singsonged. She and Darcy lifted Molly to her feet between the steel bars.

"Everything hurts," Molly moaned.

"Hi, girls," Mrs. Mason said, walking briskly into the room. She leaned over and kissed her daughter on the cheek. "How are you doing?"

"Ducky," Molly said tersely.

Mrs. Mason turned to Darcy. "Gomez and I thought we'd drive you to work ourselves today, so we canceled your car. He's waiting in front of the hospital."

Darcy looked at her watch, surprised at how late it was.

"Hello, ladies," came a lilting Jamaican voice. It belonged to Sheila Coverton, a large, beautiful black woman who was Pixie's assistant in the physical therapy room. She always came on just as Darcy was leaving.

"Hi, Molly, looking good!" Sheila said, winking at Molly. She came around on Molly's left and took over for Darcy.

"Hi, Sheila," Molly managed through her pain-tensed mouth. "Are we having fun yet?"

Darcy stepped away from the bars and pushed some stray hairs out of her face. "Gee, Mrs. Mason, you don't have to drive me—" Darcy began.

"I've been meaning to ask you, please call me Caroline," Mrs. Mason said. "And we want to drive you. It's no trouble."

"Okay, then," Darcy said with a shrug. "See you tomorrow, Molly. Call me tonight if you want to talk."

"I'll be back in a little while, sweetheart," Molly's mother told her, then she and Darcy hurried toward the front door of the hospital.

"This is really nice of you," Darcy was saying as she pushed through the main door. And then she stopped dead in her tracks and stared at the Masons' car. "You drive a hearse?"

"Why, yes," Caroline responded, as if driving a hearse were the most natural thing in the world. "We also have a BMW," she added, and held open the back door of the car for Darcy.

"Hi, Darcy, how are you?" Mr. Mason asked pleasantly as he pulled the car around the circular drive of the hospital and out into the street.

"Fine," Darcy answered distractedly. She twisted around to study the vehicle, and found herself looking at the gathered gray curtain that separated her from where the casket would be. *Very weird.*

"Is this car from one of your movies?" Darcy asked, remembering that Molly's parents were horror movie writers.

"That's right," Caroline Mason replied. "It was used in *Blood, Brains, and Barbecues*, and then we got a great price on it."

"Gee, I missed that movie," Darcy said faintly.

"I still get upset when I think about that one," Gomez Mason sighed. "Caroline and I had written the greatest scene in the script—a bunch of redneck racists at a picnic, and their bodies get hacked to death right over the barbecue pit," he recalled fondly.

"We always try to be socially aware in our scripts," Caroline told Darcy with a pleasant smile.

"The director cut the scene, said it was too controversial," Gomez fumed. "It would have made horror history!" He turned the car down Everly Boulevard and headed toward the ferry dock.

"We didn't ask to drive you to talk about our movies, however," Mrs. Mason told Darcy. "We wanted to talk about Molly."

"How is she doing, would you say?" Mr. Mason asked.

"It's hard to say," Darcy answered.

"You're the only one she seems to talk to," Molly's mother explained. "She's shutting us out, and all of her friends, too."

"Except you," Mr. Mason added.

"Yes, except you," Mrs. Mason agreed. "She's so very angry. . . ."

"Well, wouldn't you be?" Darcy asked.

"Yes, I'm sure I would be," Mrs. Mason said. "And if I could possibly trade places with her, I'd do it."

"I can't tell you things she's told me in

confidence," Darcy said, feeling uncomfortable. "It just wouldn't be right."

Caroline sighed. "I understand. It's just that her doctor says she could be progressing more rapidly, but she doesn't seem to want to. We thought you might have some insight. . . ."

"I really think Molly has to work it out herself," Darcy said earnestly. "She doesn't have to progress on anyone else's timetable—"

"It's just not like Molly to not want to do the best she can," Molly's father interrupted. "She's always been a fighter."

"But this is different!" Darcy cried. "She's still a fighter, but this isn't like shooting the rapids or . . . or jumping out of a plane. Her life has been completely turned upside down!"

"Yes, that's what her psychologist says," Mrs. Mason agreed. "We just want so much to help."

"I think you're probably doing everything you can do right now," Darcy said gently. "Don't pressure her. She doesn't want to disappoint you because she loves you."

"It's very difficult to do that, as you might

imagine," Gomez Mason said. "Which is why we're coming to you."

"We've given this a lot of thought," Caroline said, turning to look at Darcy. "We have a proposition for you. As you know, Molly is coming home in a few days, and she'll be at the physical therapy center on an outpatient basis. We'd like to offer you a job as her companion."

"A job?" Darcy echoed.

"You'd live with us—we've got a huge, old house, so you'd have your own room and privacy," Mrs. Mason continued. "We'd give you room and board and two hundred dollars a week."

"You don't have to offer me a job!" Darcy said quickly. "I'll come spend time with Molly just like I have been!" She felt embarrassed, as if they were buying her attention to their daughter.

"We know you and Molly have gotten really close," Gomez said. "But you can't go on spending every single day, all of your free time, nursing Molly. Eventually the time will taper off; it's just human!"

Darcy bit her lower lip and didn't answer. *Would my time with Molly eventually taper off?* she wondered. *Would I start to find*

excuses to miss a day here, and day there,
until I felt so guilty that I'd stop going to see
her at all?

"It's just that you do so well with her, we really believe she'll be happiest and progress the quickest with you around," Caroline said earnestly. She gave her husband a quick glance. He looked back at her and nodded. "Also," Caroline continued, "I hope this isn't too personal, but Molly told us about your financial problems, and how you don't know if you'll be able to afford college. . . ."

Darcy's face burned with embarrassment. Molly had no right to share that information with her parents!

"If you decide to accept this job, we'll also pay your college tuition at the University of Maine—you could easily commute from our house."

Darcy's jaw fell open. For a moment she was speechless. "You're offering to pay for me to go to college?" she asked, in a hushed voice.

"That's right," Gomez agreed. "You could think of it as a scholarship. The fact of the matter is, we can afford to do it, and we'd like to help you in return for your helping our daughter."

114

Darcy's mind was whirling around at a thousand miles per hour. This seemed like the opportunity of a lifetime! She'd really be able to go to college! And with her room and board and tuition covered, two hundred dollars a week would go far—she could even help out her family financially! But how could she benefit from Molly's accident when she felt so responsible for it? How could she do it?

Gomez pulled the car into the ferry dock, and turned around to look at Darcy. "We hope you'll accept."

Darcy gulped hard. "I'm . . . I don't know what to say," she stammered. "I've got to think about this."

"Certainly." Caroline nodded. "Give it a lot of thought. But we really hope you decide to do this."

"Does Molly know about this?" Darcy asked.

"It was Molly's idea," Gomez said quietly.

"Thank you," Darcy said, getting out of the hearse. "I'll call you tonight." She was in such a daze as she walked into Sweet Stuff that she didn't even notice the gawkers staring at the pearl gray hearse as it sped off down the road.

EIGHT

"But, Darcy, I don't want you to go!" Lilly cried, hugging her pillow to her on the bed.

"I'm not going far, sweetie," Darcy told her as she shoved some more T-shirts into her suitcase.

It was a week later, and Darcy was doing her final packing to move to the Masons' house on Sunset Island. It hadn't taken her long to decide that what the Masons were offering might be the opportunity of a lifetime. Once she was back at Sweet Stuff, Summer began ordering her around once again. Knowing that her uncle was sending Summer to college instead of her, watching her uncle coyly playing kissy-face with Summer's mom, well, it was all kind of sickening. As soon as she'd arrived home from work that day, she'd told her parents about the extraordinary offer the Masons had made.

Once Darcy had made it clear that the offer was genuine, her parents had been completely supportive of her taking the job. Her mother, in fact, considered it a godsend—now Darcy would actually be able to go to college! To her father Darcy had confessed her anxiety over profiting from Molly's accident, but he had convinced her not to look at it that way.

"What's done can't be undone, daughter," he'd told her when they had a private moment, "and you'll be helping Molly just as she's helping you."

"Will you write me letters?" Lilly asked sorrowfully. "Mommy will read them to me."

Darcy bent down in front of her little sister and hugged her. "Honey, I'm not moving far away. I'll come back home lots."

"But why do you have to move there?" Lilly asked, her eyes filling with tears.

"It's a job," Darcy explained. "I'm going to help take care of my friend Molly, who got hurt in an accident."

"If I get hurted in an accident, will you come take care of me?" Lilly asked, her lower lip trembling.

"Nothing bad is going to happen to you, ever," Darcy said fiercely, hugging the little girl hard until she squirmed to be released. Darcy walked over to her dresser and took a star-shaped rhinestone pin out of her small jewelry box. "Maybe you could hold on to this for me," Darcy said, handing it to Lilly.

"I could wear it?" Lilly asked, her eyes wide. Darcy collected rhinestone pins, and the star had always been Lilly's favorite.

"Yes, but Mom has to pin it on for you, and you have to put it back in the jewelry box after every time you wear it," Darcy said solemnly.

"Yo, let's book!" Dean yelled upstairs. He was driving Darcy to Sunset Island before his shift at the shipyard.

"Just a sec!" Darcy yelled back down. She threw the last pile of clothes into the suitcase, and shut the lid. It was so ancient, it only snapped shut on one side, and Darcy only hoped it wouldn't spring open as she carried it downstairs.

"Come on, I gotta hustle or I'll be late for work," Dean said, grabbing the suitcase from Darcy and carrying it out to the car.

"Can I come?" Lilly asked, staring up at her brother.

"Sorry, squirt, not this time," Dean said, tousling Lilly's dark curls.

"All set?" Darcy's father asked, limping into the living room.

Darcy nodded, looking around at the shabby house. A lump formed in her throat. It wasn't that she loved her house—in fact, she hated it—but she did love the people who lived there. It was home, and she was leaving for the very first time.

"Now, now, none of that," Connor Laken grumbled, seeing the tears welling up in Darcy's eyes. "You'll come home for Sunday supper—that's only a few days from now."

"If I can," Darcy said. "'Bye, dad." She hugged her father, hugged Lilly again, and went out to the car.

"So aren't you the lucky one," Dean said as he drove down the street, "moving out of our happy hellhole."

"Don't call it that," Darcy snapped. "Mom and Dad do the best they can."

"Yeah, sure," Dean grunted.

"Let's see you do better," Darcy taunted him, her temper flaring. Dean was the sibling she got along with the least. Lately he always seemed to have a chip on his shoulder. Only two years ahead of her in school, he'd resented it when she'd won a place at Kennedy, while he'd had to attend the ill-equipped, often dangerous local public school. Dean had hated school so much, in fact, that he'd dropped out halfway through his senior year. No amount of screaming or pleading by his parents could force him back. Darcy thought it was a shame, because Dean was really very smart. His dead-end job at the Bath shipyard would never make use of his brains.

"I plan to do better, little girl," Dean said. "Wait and see."

"How do you plan to accomplish that without going back to school?" Darcy asked practically.

"There are ways," Dean said vaguely.

"All you have to do is go for your GED, and then we could go to college together," Darcy said.

Dean stopped at a light and looked at Darcy. "With what bucks, Dar? Not everyone lucks into a free ride like you just did."

"It isn't a free ride," Darcy shot back. "It's . . . Oh, just forget it." It was pointless to try to talk with Dean when he was in one of his nasty moods. Darcy stared out the window and was soon lost in thought, dreaming about what college would be like.

After the ferry across to the island, Darcy read the directions Caroline had given her to get to the Masons' house. "We take a right on Winding Road," Darcy said, reading from the paper. "There should be a light there."

"Nice digs," Dean commented as he took the turn. They were in a lovely neighborhood of manicured lawns upon which sat palatial summer homes.

"Okay, we should come to a fork in the road coming up," Darcy said. "We go left. Then we'll see a huge hill to the right."

"This must be it," Dean said, veering the car to the left. "And that must be the hill."

"Molly's mother said you could see their house from the bottom of the hill," Darcy said, peering upward. "Oh my God, is that it?"

Way up above them, set on what looked to be the edge of the hill, was a cavernous-looking house that looked to be straight out of a gothic horror story.

"Turn there." Darcy pointed. "That's their private road."

The car bumped along up the winding gravel road, until they stopped in front of the house.

"This place looks haunted," Dean said, staring at the huge house.

Darcy was speechless. She remembered Molly telling her that the house was, as Molly put it, "hilarious," but she hadn't expected this. The house looked ancient and forbidding. The windows were framed by black shutters, some of which blew back and forth in the light breeze. The front door, also black, was at least ten feet high. Darcy looked up and saw a circular balcony running around the uppermost part of the house. She gasped when she realized there was a skeleton hanging over the balcony, one hand up as if in midwave.

"You could do a great production of *The Rocky Horror Picture Show* here," Dean observed, mesmerized by the house. He looked at his sister. "Are you sure this is cool, Dar? Because we can turn right around and I can take you home, if you want."

"No, it's okay—I think," Darcy added under her breath. She got out of the car and lugged her suitcase up to the front door. Dean carried the large box full of stuff that made up the rest of her belongings.

"You want me to wait?" Dean asked, setting the box down next to Darcy.

"No, I'm fine, and you'll be late for work," Darcy said. She reached up to knock on the door and pulled her hand away quickly. The door knocker was in the shape of a skull.

"I'm definitely not leaving you here until I check this out," Dean said, staring at the skull door knocker.

Darcy knocked on the door, which was opened quickly by a very tall, very thin man in a tuxedo. His face was so gaunt-looking that he was almost cadaverous.

"You rang?" he growled, peering down at Darcy and Dean.

He's got to be seven feet tall, Darcy thought, staring up at the man. *Dean's six three, and this guy towers over him. He also looks like he hasn't eaten in days.* "I'm Darcy Laken," Darcy said, attempting a smile. "This is my brother Dean."

The skeletal man looked Darcy over, nodding slowly, then looked at Dean. "Hello, Darcy, hello, brother Dean."

"I'm . . . I'm supposed to be moving in here, to, uh, work." Darcy stammered, flustered. She peered past the man, hoping for a glimpse of Molly or her parents, but all she saw was a huge, empty front hall and a circular staircase.

"Yeeees, we've been expecting you," the man said, nodding once again. "I am Simon, the butler, at your service." He gave a small bow, a sinister smile playing along the corners of his mouth.

"Uh, what exactly is the deal here?" Dean asked. "I mean, no offense, but you look like you just stepped out of 'The Addams Family'. You look like that butler dude, Merch or something."

"I believe you mean Lurch," Simon corrected him, "and I thank you from the bottom of my hideously beating heart for the compliment."

Dean cocked his head to one side. "This is a joke, right? I mean, you want to look like this Lurch character?"

"He is nothing less than my hero," Simon intoned in his deep, gravelly voice.

Dean turned to Darcy. "Sis, we are outta here—"

"No, it's okay," Darcy assured him, hoping that it really was. "Molly's parents write horror movies; they're just kind of . . . into this stuff. And I guess you are, too, right, Simon?"

"I am a horror movie thespian of the first order, madam," Simon said, "forced to struggle as a butler between meaningful acting engagements."

"See?" Darcy told her brother. "No problem. "He's an actor!"

"Oh, brother," Dean mumbled.

"Darcy, you're here!" Caroline called, appearing at the top of the stairs. "I'm so sorry I couldn't greet you—I got stuck on a call to the coast."

Once again, Darcy stood there dumbfounded. Because Caroline Mason didn't look anything like the Caroline Mason she'd spent so much time with over the past two weeks. An attractive woman in her early forties, Caroline had had her dark hair up in a chignon, and had worn regular clothes and little makeup every time Darcy had seen her. But at the top of the stairs stood an entirely different woman.

Caroline's long, black hair—almost as long as Darcy's—fell straight from a center part. The palest of skin powder served as an eerie contrast to heavily lined eyes and bloodred lips. And then there was her dress. She had on a black, floor-length dress, cut very low in the front, with see-through mesh spiderweb netting that ran to her neck. The sleeves of the dress came to a long point over each wrist, leading to fingers featuring the longest, reddest nails Darcy had ever seen. And in one hand, she held a glittery, black cigarette holder.

"Hi," Darcy said, her voice squeaking as she stared at Caroline gracefully making her way down the circular stairway. "Uh, this is my brother Dean. This is Caroline Mason."

"Charmed," Caroline said, holding out her hand to Dean. He shook it, a dazed look on his face.

"You look . . . different," Darcy managed.

"Yes I suppose I do," Caroline agreed. "When Molly was in the hospital, I felt it would be better to wear that dreary suburban costume. I'm just thankful that she's home now and I can really relax!"

Dean leaned in close to Darcy. "Are you sure you don't want to make a run for it?"

"Everything's fine," Darcy assured him.

"Well, I have to go to work," Dean said, looking dubiously at Caroline and Simon. "You call home tonight, you understand?" he told his sister.

"I will," Darcy promised. She hugged her brother, and he left.

"So, Simon will show you your room—it's just down the hall from Molly's," Caroline said. "She's in her room, napping. She's been so excited that you decided to take this job."

"Well, I'm excited about it, too," Darcy said.

"After you're settled, say in an hour, why don't you meet me in the kitchen, and we'll have a talk, okay?"

"Fine," Darcy agreed, and she followed Simon up the long, winding stairs.

"Your room," Simon growled, and ushered Darcy in. She looked around at the huge oak canopy bed covered in a mulicolored quilt, the gleaming, highly polished hardwood floor, and the tapestry area rug, and she fell in love. It was a large and airy room, substantially bigger than the cramped room she shared at home. Best of all, it was uncluttered. After living with eight people in a small house, Darcy craved open space. "It's terrific," Darcy said.

"You'll find your bathroom through that door," Simon said, pointing. "If you need anything, let me know."

"Thanks," Darcy said as Simon bowed slightly and walked out of the room.

Darcy opened the closet door, and was pleasantly surprised to find a huge walk-in closet. Then she opened the bathroom door, and let out a whoop. The bathroom was ultra–modern and featured mirrored tiles and a huge sunken bathtub.

"Too cool!" Darcy screamed, jumping into the empty tub from sheer happiness. Back at the Laken house there was only one bathroom, featuring an ancient bathtub and limited hot water. Four people could fit in this bathtub at the same time! *Not that I know anyone I'd want to take a bath with,* Darcy thought with a laugh, *except maybe Mark Greyson!*

Darcy snapped her suitcase open and started to put her clothes into the oak dresser. She didn't have many, so it didn't take very long. She hung her few skirts and dresses and jeans in the huge closet, arranged her shoes neatly in a row, and put her toiletries in the bathroom. Then she unpacked the box of personal things, and set a framed family photo from her high school graduation on the dressing table. "Home, sweet home," she murmured, and decided to go look for Molly.

Darcy heard the strains of Wylie and the Wild West Show, a very hot country band from Los Angeles, coming from a room down the hall. She went and knocked on the door.

"Come on in," Molly called. She was sitting

in her wheelchair, staring out the window into the forest beyond the house.

"Hi," Darcy said. "Want company?"

"That's what they're paying you for, isn't it?" Molly asked. The cassette finished, and silence filled the room. Molly stared at Darcy, waiting for her answer.

"I thought you wanted me to be here," Darcy finally said.

Molly shrugged and turned back to the window.

"If you really don't want me here, I'll go," Darcy said. "Just say the word."

"I don't care," Molly mumbled.

"Look, I'm not going to lie to you," Darcy said slowly, pushing her hair behind her ear. "This is a great opportunity for me. But I kind of thought maybe we could help each other."

"I don't want to need any help," Molly said in a low voice.

"Neither do I," Darcy agreed, "but I do."

"Just don't expect me to be nice all the time, or pleasant, or a good sport," Molly spat out.

"Deal," Darcy nodded.

Molly bit her lip. "I'm just . . . afraid that if you work here, we won't really be friends anymore. And I think maybe you're the only friend I have left."

Darcy crossed the room swiftly and hugged Molly tight. "I'm your friend, no matter what," she vowed.

Molly wiped her eyes with the back of her hand. "Enough of this mush," she said, taking a deep breath. "What do you think of the house? Mondo-bizarro, huh?"

"It's the strangest place I've ever seen," Darcy said honestly. "Simon is a riot! And your mom is dressed like she'd auditioning for one of her own movies!"

"She says it helps her write," Molly said, rolling her eyes. "That's why my dad changed his name to Gomez, too. It used to be plain old Edward."

"Unbelievable," Darcy said, leaning back against Molly's desk. "I was wondering about that."

"Careful, you're leaning on my police report," Molly said.

Darcy moved the papers and scanned them briefly. "This is the statement you made about your accident?"

Molly nodded, taking the papers from Darcy. "They wanted me to read it over again, to see if I remember anything."

"And do you?" Darcy asked.

"Not a thing," Molly admitted. "The last thing I remember is driving down the road, wondering what I should wear to a party that night, and then I don't remember anything until I woke up in the hospital."

"And there were no witnesses at all?" Darcy asked.

"Not one," Molly said with a sigh. "Sometimes I feel as if I can almost remember something, as if it's just right beyond my grasp, and then even that feeling slips away."

"Well, I, for one, hope you remember," Darcy told her. "I can't stand the thought that someone got away with hurting you."

"That's how my dad feels, too," Molly said. "But I don't know. I mean, what difference would it make? Catching the jerk wouldn't help me walk again, would it?"

"I suppose not," Darcy admitted. "But I just can't live with injustice. I never could."

"Me, neither," said Molly. She looked down at her lifeless legs. "But this is one injustice that I'm going to have to live with. Forever."

NINE

"No! Nooooooooo! Help me!"

Darcy woke up with a start, her heart pounding in her chest. Had she really heard that or had it been a dream?

"Noooooooooo!"

It was Molly! Darcy ran down the hall and into Molly's room. Molly was sitting up in bed, rocking and crying.

"Shhhhh, it's okay, I'm right here," Darcy said, wrapping her arms around Molly.

"I had the most terrible nightmare," Molly managed to gasp between sobs. "I dreamt about the accident. I was right there, going through it again; it was so terrible. . . ."

"It's okay now," Darcy crooned. "You're safe now."

"I remember screaming, and then I was flying through the air," Molly sobbed. "And then I remember lying on the street, staring up at the sky. I was so scared. And a face leaned over me, a guy with blond hair. I think he was crying, but his face was a blur because something was in my eyes, and then he was gone. And I was all alone!"

Darcy held Molly until she stopped crying and calmed down. "Okay now?" she asked.

Molly nodded and took a deep, shuddery breath. "Okay," she finally said.

"You remembered something," Darcy prodded gently. "A guy with blond hair . . . ?"

"That's all," Molly said. "I don't want to remember; it's too horrible." She lay back down in her bed.

"Can you sleep now?"

Molly nodded mutely.

"Good night, then," Darcy said, getting up from the bed. "If you need me, just call." She shut the door and hurried down to her own room. As she fell back asleep, she hoped that more memories would come back to Molly. *I want to get the bastard*, she thought sleepily, and nestled back down into the covers. *I really, really want to get him.*

The next morning at breakfast, Darcy told Molly's parents about the dream. Since their room was in the other wing, they hadn't heard Molly's screams.

"Well, let's hope this is only the beginning," Gomez said, pouring himself another cup of coffee.

"But if the memories are so frightening for her, perhaps she'd be better off not reliving it," Caroline pointed out.

"Maybe," Darcy mused. She looked over at Molly's parents as she buttered a piece of toast. Caroline had on a red silk dressing gown with a large, black snake embroidered around the sleeve, and Gomez wore a black silk dressing gown over black pants, with red velvet slippers. They were about as different from her parents as two people could be, and yet they loved Molly with the same intensity that her parents loved her. *You sure can't tell a book by its cover*, Darcy thought.

"Molly rang," Simon said, walking soundlessly into the kitchen. Molly parents had had an in-house intercom system installed so that Molly could call into any room at any time.

"I'll take her breakfast up," Darcy said, swallowing the last of her coffee.

"I shall make up a tray," Simon said gravely.

"Marvella can do it," Caroline said. "I just heard her come in. Marvella is our house-keeper," Caroline explained to Darcy.

"Marvella overacts," Simon sniffed. "And I'll get Molly's tray. I know what she likes."

"Marvella and Simon used to be an item," Gomez explained after Simon went into the kitchen. "She used to be an actress—maybe you saw her in *Hatchet Harlots from Hell*?"

"Missed that one," Darcy said, stifling a laugh.

"Too bad, she died brilliantly," Gomez reminisced. "Anyway, she left the business and married a lovely guy who makes rubber scars, fake blood, that kind of thing. Simon has never gotten over it."

"Here it is, everything Molly likes," Simon said, handing Darcy the tray.

"I wish she'd decide to come down and eat with us," Caroline sighed. "She hasn't eaten a meal down here since she got home."

"She hates the idea of being carried down, madam," Simon said with dignity. "Perhaps when the elevator is installed."

Darcy took the tray upstairs, knocking

with her foot and then sailing into the room. "Hi, how'd you sleep?"

"Okay," Molly replied. "No more bad dreams, anyway."

"Do you remember what you told me?"

"About the guy with the blond hair?" Molly asked, picking up her fruit cup. "Yeah, I do."

"Do you think maybe we should tell the police?" Darcy asked. "I mean, it's a new piece of information."

"Good idea," Molly replied, spooning some cantaloupe and berries into her mouth. "How about in an hour?"

"Sure, we can call in an hour," Darcy agreed.

"Well, we could, but it seems pointless when the policeman will be standing right here." Molly spread some honey on her toast and licked a dribble off her finger. "I already called them. Sergeant something-or-other—I forget his name—is coming over."

"Great!" Darcy said with surprise.

"It's only my legs that don't work," Molly said archly, wiggling her hand at Darcy. "I let my fingers do the walking."

After breakfast, Darcy helped Molly shower and dress, then she ran quickly to her own room and went through her own morning ritual. By the time Darcy was pulling up her jeans, Simon was calling her over the intercom. "A visitor in blue, madam," he grumbled through the phone.

Darcy took a last swipe at her hair—she hadn't had time to wash it—and bounded down the stairs.

"Good morning, miss, I'm Sergeant Phillips," the young policeman said, reaching out his hand to Darcy.

"Darcy Laken—I'm Molly's friend," Darcy replied, shaking his hand firmly. She immediately noticed how cute he was—a fact that would be hard to miss. Well over six feet tall, with broad shoulders and a slender torso, Sergeant Phillips had sandy blond hair and bright blue eyes. With his serious, earnest expression and that cleft in his chin, he reminded Darcy of someone, but she couldn't put her finger on who it was.

"I understand Miss Mason has had some memory return about her accident," he said gravely, pulling out a pad and a pen.

"Yes, she's upstairs," Darcy said. "Follow me."

Sergeant Phillips stole a look at Simon, who gave him his most ghoulish grin, and then he hurried up the stairs after Darcy.

"Hello, Miss Mason, nice to see you again," Officer Phillips said, nodding curtly at Molly.

"Have a seat," Molly told him. "As you can see, I've already had one."

"I understand you have something you want to add to the statement you gave me in the hospital," the policeman said.

Molly went through what she remembered, and the officer took it all down.

"Can you describe the man who bent over you?" Sergeant Phillips asked.

"It was blurry; something was in my eyes," Molly said.

Darcy grimaced. It had to have been the blood that had run copiously from a gash on Molly's forehead.

"Did he say anything?" the policeman pressed. "Anything at all?"

"I think he was crying," Molly said. "That's really all I remember."

Sergeant Phillips read Molly's statement back to her. "Is that it?"

"Yes," Molly confirmed, then a startled look came over her face. "Wait! I remember, I turned my head slightly, I was so afraid to have him leave me, and he was running! I remember him running away!"

The policeman was silent for a moment.

"You remember him leaving the scene of the crime?"

"I saw him running away from me!" Molly cried painfully.

Sergeant Phillips closed his notebook and stood up. "I'm sorry to have had to put you through this. I'd really like to catch this guy."

"My sentiments exactly," Darcy agreed. "I'll walk you downstairs." She put her hand on Molly's shoulder, which trembled under her fingers. "I'll be right back," she said softly.

"Man, this is one perp I'd love to nail," Sergeant Phillips said when he and Darcy reached the front hall. "In my book, the guy is total scum."

"In mine, too," Darcy agreed.

Sergeant Phillips looked at Darcy with curiosity. "You're her friend, you said?"

"And her companion, I guess you'd call it."

"She seems like a great kid," the policeman said.

"She is," Darcy agreed. "I'm lucky to have her as a friend."

Sergeant Phillips looked Darcy over shyly. "So, do you live here?"

"Yeah, as of yesterday," Darcy said. "Before that I lived in Portland with my family."

"So you don't know the island, then?" he asked

"Not much," Darcy said. "My uncle owns Sweet Stuff, and I worked there for a few weeks. I've been to the beach a couple of times—that's about it."

"Well, it's a great place; you should get out and see it."

"I'm sure Molly will show me around," Darcy said.

"Yes. Well . . ." Sergeant Phillips began, shifting his weight from foot to foot.

Why, he wants to ask me out! Darcy suddenly realized. *He wants to, but he's too shy!*

"I'll call you in a few days," he said. The policeman fumbled with his hat. "I mean, I'll call *here* in a few days, to see if Miss Mason remembers anything else."

"Fine," Darcy agreed.

"Well, nice to meet you, Miss Laken," Sergeant Phillips said formally.

"Call me Darcy," Darcy said. "Do you have a first name, or is it 'Sergeant'?"

"It's Scott," the sergeant said with a boyish grin.

"Okay, well, thanks, Scott," Darcy said, shaking hands.

"I hope to see you again soon," he said. He tipped his cap and headed out the door.

Very cute, Darcy thought, watching him walk away, *but a serious straight arrow if ever I've met one.* Just as she was turning away to go back upstairs to Molly, she saw Rowena and Jenny getting out of a Miata convertible.

"Hi," Rowena called as they walked up to the front door. "I hope it's okay that we stopped over; Molly hasn't returned any of my calls."

"I'm sure she'll be glad to see you guys," Darcy assured them. "Let me run up and tell her you're here."

"You okay?" Darcy asked Molly softly when she got back up to the bedroom. Molly was staring out the window, something she seemed to spend a great deal of time doing.

"It's so weird, remembering," Molly said. "It's as if I'm telling you about a movie, instead of about something that actually happened to me."

"I know it's hard," Darcy said, "but your memory is the only key that we have to catching the guy. Hey, guess who's downstairs? Rowena and Jenny!"

Molly shot a quick look at Darcy. "I didn't invite them over."

"You didn't answer their phone calls, either."

"Maybe I didn't want to answer their phone calls," Molly shot back. "As far as I know, I still have free will, right?"

"But they're your friends," Darcy said softly. "They care about you."

"Look, I'm not going to pretend I want to see them, even though that's what everyone wants me to do," Molly said adamantly. "I just . . . I just can't right now."

"If you push them away for too long, you might push them so far that they won't come back," Darcy warned.

"I'd rather be alone than pitied," Molly snapped.

"Who says they—" Darcy began.

"You promised you wouldn't do this!" Molly interrupted. "You said you wouldn't tell me how I should feel or what I should do!"

Darcy bit her lower lip. "Okay, Molly you're right." Darcy understood that Molly felt as if one of the only things she had left was her will, and respecting that was all-important. "I'll go tell them you don't want company right now."

"Can we go up?" Jenny asked, getting up from the couch in the living room where the two girls were waiting.

"She doesn't want company right now," Darcy said. "I'm really sorry you drove over for nothing."

"I just don't understand her," Rowena said, shaking her head. "If it were me, I'd be happy that my friends still wanted to be my friends!"

"No offense," Darcy said, "but you don't really know *how* you'd feel."

"Well, aside from turning into a hermit, how's she doing?" Jenny asked.

"Okay," Darcy said. "She's still spending the afternoons at the hospital in physical therapy—in fact, I have to take her over there soon. Oh, and last night she remembered something about the accident—a guy with blond hair bending over her after she'd been thrown from the car. She says she thinks he was crying, and she remembers him running away."

"God, that's awful." Rowena shuddered.

"Oh, I almost forgot," Jenny said, pulling a

white envelope out of her purse. "This card is for Molly, from Andy."

"The Andy she was dating?" Darcy asked with surprise, taking the card. "The one who sent the flowers to the hospital?"

Jenny nodded. "I saw him last night at a party, and he asked me to give that to Molly."

"Why couldn't he just deliver it himself?" Darcy asked with disgust.

"He's really busy," Jenny said. "He's helping with his dad's reelection campaign for mayor."

"Too busy to visit his girlfriend after she had a terrible car accident?" Darcy scoffed. "Give me a break!"

Jenny blushed. "Well, Molly wasn't exactly his girlfriend," she mumbled. "They just hung out a few times."

In a flash, Darcy knew what the truth was. And she didn't think it was because she was psychic, either. "You didn't just happen to see Andy at a party last night," Darcy said, staring hard at Jenny. "You went to the party with him, didn't you?"

"Well, like I said, they really weren't a couple," Jenny said defensively.

Darcy looked at Rowena. "Were you

there, too? Were you going to tell Molly the truth?"

"Jenny has a right to go out with him," Rowena said. "I mean, what difference does it make now? Molly's in a wheelchair!"

Darcy's fists clenched hard. "You think that because she's in a wheelchair, a guy wouldn't like her anymore?"

"You can pretend it doesn't make any difference," Jenny said, standing her ground, "and maybe it shouldn't, but it does."

It was everything Darcy could do to not punch Jenny in her earnest face. "Get out of here," she finally told them, and turned and went back upstairs.

"We're still her friends, Darcy, whether you believe it or not," Rowena called up.

But Darcy just ignored her, and kept on going.

TEN

"I don't want to go back downstairs," Molly said adamantly. "I want to finish reading this book."

"Come on, let me take you down," Darcy wheedled. "Your parents have a surprise for you."

It was three days later, and just an hour earlier, Darcy and Molly had returned from Molly's physical therapy at the hospital. As usual, Molly wanted to hole up in her room and be left alone, and Darcy was trying to talk her out of it.

"Tell them to come up here and tell the surprise, then," Molly said, opening her book up again.

"It's not a tell-you-type surprise, it's a show-you-type surprise. And it can't be brought upstairs," Darcy explained.

"Okay, okay," Molly sighed, putting her book down. She let Darcy pick her up and carry her downstairs. Fortunately Molly was small and slender—even more slender than before her accident—and Darcy could easily carry her.

"Close your eyes," Darcy said as they reached the front hall.

"This is incredibly stupid," Molly groused, but she obediently shut her eyes, anyway.

Darcy carried her out the front door, where Simon had already set up a chair. She set Molly in the chair, traded smiles with Gomez and Caroline, and told Molly to open her eyes.

"Wow!" Molly said. She was staring at a brand-new cherry red van with a huge white ribbon wrapped all the way around the body. On the license plate was the name "Molly."

"Do you love it, darling?" Caroline asked eagerly.

"It's . . . it's great," Molly said in a faltering voice.

"The back is specially designed for your wheelchair!" Molly's father told her enthusiastically. "There's even a hydraulic lift to make it easier to get the chair in and out!"

"It's a really nice surprise," Molly said,

staring desolately at the ground. "Too bad the owner will never be able to drive it."

"Wrong!" Darcy cried excitedly. "The van is equipped with special hand brakes and hand gas pedals—all you have to do is learn to use them and then pass a test, and you've got wheels, girl!"

Molly's jaw fell open. "Really?" she asked hopefully. "Is that really true?"

"It's completely true, sweetheart!" Gomez assured her.

"Allow me to put you in the driver's seat," Simon said, gently lifting Molly and carrying her over to the car.

"This is awesome!" Molly cried, putting her hands on the steering wheel. "And I'm really going to be able to drive it?"

"We spoke with a young man from the Spinal Cord Injury Foundation who has the same injury you have," Caroline told her daughter. "As soon as you give the word, he's ready to come over and teach you to drive your van!"

"Short of working legs, this is the very best gift you could have given me," Molly said softly.

"If we could give you your first choice, you know we would," Caroline said quietly.

"Hey, how about if we go for a spin?" Darcy asked Molly. "The van can also be driven with the regular foot pedals."

"Great!" Molly agreed. Darcy moved Molly over to the passenger side, and slid into the driver's seat.

"We'll see you when we see you," Molly said airily, waving to her parents out her window. "I love you!" she yelled as Darcy pulled the van away from the house.

"I can't believe I'm going to be able to drive again!" Molly told Darcy. "I never thought it would be possible."

"This guy, Jason, from the Spinal Cord Injury Foundation told me there's all kinds of things you can do, if you want to," Darcy said as she drove.

"It's just that driving will give me so much freedom," Molly mused. "That's the main thing."

"We can call him when we get back if you want," Darcy said, "and set up your first driving lesson."

"I can't wait!" Molly yelled. She flipped on the radio, and the sounds of Michael Bolton filled the car. She closed her eyes and let the wind rush through her hair, a blissful expression on her face. Darcy smiled at her—

this was the happiest she'd seen Molly since before the accident.

Darcy drove out into the least-populated beach area, turning at random down the empty roads. In her rearview mirror she noticed a small green sports car behind her. The same car had been behind them ever since they'd made the turn off the Masons' private road.

That's odd, Darcy thought. *Why would someone take the same circuitous route we're taking when we're not headed anywhere in particular?*

Just for fun, Darcy took a sharp left toward the beach, and sure enough, the green sports car followed her. Then she turned at the next side street in the opposite direction, onto a steep road that ran alongside a cliff, perpendicular to the beach. The green car turned with her.

"I know this is going to sound crazy," Darcy yelled over the music, "but I think someone is following us."

"They just want to see who owns such a buff van," Molly joked.

Darcy sped up and watched the green car speed up behind her. "I'm serious," she said, turning down the music so that Molly could hear her. "There's a green car—a Jaguar, I think—that's definitely following us!"

Molly twisted around as best she could, but she couldn't see behind her over the headrest on her seat. "I can't see," she said.

"Maybe if I move into the right lane and slow down, he'll just pass us on the left," Darcy muttered. She moved into the narrow right lane, which dipped steeply at the shoulder down to the beach.

Darcy watched in her rearview mirror as the green car sped up again, only this time it didn't slow down. As she watched in horror, the car came up on her tail on the left-hand side.

"He's trying to hit us!" Darcy screamed, and tried to swerve out of the green car's way. But she had no maneuvering room on the right side, and the green car was bearing down on her on the left.

Boom! The car nudged the van toward the precipice. Molly screamed, and Darcy deftly turned the wheel and managed to stay on the road. She pushed the gas pedal down hard, hoping to outrun the sport's car, but it was no use. *Boom!* The car hit her fender again. For a brief moment, Darcy lost control of the van. She skidded onto the narrow edge.

"We're going to crash!" Molly screamed.

At the last moment, Darcy was able to wrestle the van back onto the road. "Please, God, let us get out of this," she prayed as she watched the car coming toward them once again.

"Look! A turn!" Molly screamed, pointing to a narrow dirt road that led down the precipice.

Darcy turned the wheel sharply onto the dirt road. The car, which had been accelerating, zoomed past, unable to slow down in time to make the unexpected turn. Darcy drove off into a side area and parked, her hands shaking violently.

"Are you okay?" she asked Molly.

But Molly was just shaking and crying, unable to speak.

"It's all over now," Darcy said softly, stroking Molly's hair.

"All of a sudden I was back at the accident," Molly sobbed. "I thought we were going to die!"

"Whoever was driving that car is crazy or drunk or both," Darcy seethed. "We've got to report this to the police. Can you handle going over to the police station?"

"I just want to go home," Molly said. She was still shivering uncontrollably.

Darcy drove them back in silence, keeping a careful watch for the green car, but they arrived back at the Mason house without incident. Darcy carried Molly up to her room.

"I'm going to the police station," she told Molly. "Do you want me to ask your mom to come up and be with you?"

Molly shook her head. "And don't tell my parents what happened, either. They're still trying to get over the other accident. I don't want them to get upset all over again."

"Okay," Darcy agreed softly. She shut Molly's door and hurried downstairs and out to the van. Just as she was about to open the door on the driver's side, a light flashed in her head.

And she knew.

The person driving that car was the same person who had hit Molly.

Mesmerized, she stared into the distance, willing a picture of the person's face to come to her. But all she saw was darkness and fear.

Darcy hurried toward the police station, filled with anxiety. Now she didn't trust these "flashes" anymore. Because certainly she hated the unknown driver who had hit Molly and run away as much as—more than—she hated Marianne, and Marianne had turned out to be healthy. *Yes, but after your dream about Molly, she had her accident, and you did nothing to prevent it,* she reminded herself ruthlessly. *You have to say something, even if you feel like a fool.*

At the police station she asked for Sergeant Scott Phillips. He quickly came out to the lobby.

"Well, hi!" he said, his face lighting up with pleasure at seeing Darcy again.

"I have to talk to you," Darcy said urgently.

The smile fell from Scott's lips. Obviously he could see how upset Darcy was. "Come on," he said, gently steering Darcy toward a private office. He poured her a cup of coffee and handed it to her before he sat down.

"Thank you," she said, sipping at the hot, black coffee. She took a few deep breaths to gain control, and then looked up purposefully at Scott. "Someone just tried to run Molly and me off the road."

"Are you serious?" Scott asked in surprise.

"Dead serious," Darcy said. "Whoever it was wanted to kill us; I'm certain of that."

Scott looked skeptical, then pulled out his pad and pen. "Okay, before we jump to any conclusions, tell me exactly what happened."

Darcy described the vivid scene, right down to how she had barely made the turnoff to escape the green car. "If Molly hadn't seen that turn, the car would have forced us off on the right, and we'd have crashed down the cliff," Darcy finished.

"It was probably some drunk kid," Scott said. "I'll put out a call to look for the car you've described. If it makes you feel any better, I'm sure it wasn't personal."

"But it was; that's what I'm trying to tell you," Darcy insisted. "That car must have been waiting right by the Masons' private road. Whoever it was was following us."

"I think you're letting your imagination get carried away here," Scott said.

"It's not my imagination," Darcy insisted. She stared into the black pool of coffee, hoping to find the right way to explain things to Scott. "Sometimes," she said, finally looking up at him, "I just know things."

"You just know things?" Scott repeated.

Darcy nodded. "Sometimes it happens in a

dream, sometimes in a flash while I'm awake." She told Scott about some of the instances when her dreams and flashes had come true. Although she felt guilty about it, she omitted the story about Marianne, lest she injure her own credibility. And then she finished with her stories about Molly, both her car accident and what she'd felt about the person in the green car.

Scott had a skeptical look on his face. "Darcy, you understand that this is very hard for me to believe."

"I probably wouldn't believe it, either, if it wasn't me that it was happening to," Darcy admitted. "But I'm telling you the truth."

Scott got up and paced around the room, then he turned back to Darcy. "I have to deal in fact," he explained. "What you're telling me just doesn't mesh with all my training."

"Do you think I'm lying?" Darcy asked, her temper flaring.

"No, but maybe your imagination is getting carried away with you," he said gently.

"That is a really condescending thing to say," Darcy snapped, jumping up angrily.

"I'm sorry, I didn't mean it to come out that way," Scott apologized quickly. "It's just that police work is a very fact-based business."

"Well, how about all the cases where psychics have helped the police catch criminals, or find kidnap victims?" Darcy asked. "You think that was all just blind luck?"

"Nothing like that has ever been proven," Scott replied.

Darcy picked up her purse and slung it over her shoulder. "Thanks for all your help," she said sarcastically, and headed for the door.

"Darcy, wait!" Scott called.

"Forget it, just forget it," Darcy flung back at him, and headed out of the police station.

She calmed down as she drove the van back to the Masons'. *You really have to learn to control your stupid temper,* she told herself. *The reason you got so mad was because you have your own small seed of doubt about all this, and you know it.* Darcy hit the steering wheel in frustration.

One part of me wants to tell Molly everything, she thought—*about being psychic, about having a premonition about her accident, and about the person driving the green car. But the other part of me feels too awful and guilty, and maybe confession would help me but would only make Molly feel much, much worse.* She was completely lost in thought when she turned the van onto the Mason's private road.

If she hadn't been, she might have noticed the blond haired driver behind the wheel of a green Jaguar hidden behind a thicket of trees, just waiting, watching, biding his time.

ELEVEN

"So what are you going to wear tonight?" Darcy asked Molly as she applied clear nail polish to Molly's pinky.

It was a week later, and that night Molly's parents were giving their annual summer cocktail party, during which they would have a private showing of their latest horror movie. It was considered quite a coup to get invited to this party. The elite of Sunset Island embraced the Masons' eccentricity— perhaps because they were rich, successful, and in show business. Caroline and Gomez had offered to cancel it if it would make Molly uncomfortable, but she'd encouraged them to proceed with their plans. They didn't want to give the party, however, unless Molly would agree to come. So although she longed to stay up in her room, she had reluctantly allowed herself to be talked into showing up.

"How about pasties and a G-string?" Molly suggested. "Then at least people will stare at me because I'm half-naked instead of because I'm half-paralyzed."

"I guess the people who haven't seen you since the accident probably will stare at you," Darcy admitted, "but you're going to have to face them eventually." She wasn't about to lie to Molly—and besides, the few times that Molly and she had gone somewhere besides the hospital, Darcy had seen people staring.

"Who says?" Molly challenged. "I can stay up here forever and grow my hair real long, like Rapunzel. Then I'll just drop my tresses out the window for any really fine prince that happens to wander into our backyard."

"Seriously, Mol, let's figure out what we're going to wear tonight. You've been to this bash every year, so tell me what's appropriate," Darcy said, screwing the cap on the nail polish.

"Well, the local gentry come in costume— your usual horror-movie-type monsters and stuff," Molly said. "Mom and Dad, of course, dress like they always dress—only more so."

"And how do you dress?" Darcy asked.

"Normal," Molly said flatly. "I've never worn a costume in the five years that they've been giving this shindig. I'll just wear jeans."

"Oh, okay," Darcy said, "then I'll just wear jeans, too." She was relieved not to have to get dressed up, because although she had a few skirts, the only dress she owned was from her high school graduation. And whenever she looked at it, it made her think of Marianne Reed. She felt more comfortable in jeans, anyway.

"Did my parents mention if Andy is coming?" Molly asked, obviously trying hard to sound casual. She waved her hands around to dry her nail polish.

"I don't know," Darcy said. *I doubt it*, she added in her head, *since he's now dating your dear friend Jenny*.

"I keep thinking maybe he's just really busy, you know?" Molly told Darcy. "And that's why I haven't seen him. I mean, he sent that card and everything, but it was hard to tell."

"Uh-huh," Darcy replied noncommittally. She couldn't bring herself to tell Molly the truth about Andy, not after everything else Molly had been through.

"You know how sometimes you just know that a relationship is special?" Molly asked Darcy. "I mean, even if you've only been out with the guy a few times?"

"Maybe you should just forget about him," Darcy said softly.

"Because he couldn't love a girl in a wheelchair?"

"No," Darcy replied, "because maybe he just isn't as special a guy as you thought he was."

"What makes you say that?" Molly asked sharply. "You never even met him."

Darcy didn't want to point out that Andy still hadn't called or visited, and she also didn't want to tell Molly about Jenny, so she deftly changed the subject.

"Andy's parents are coming; I know that," Darcy said. "I saw their names on Simon's list."

"Well, of course his parents are coming," Molly said dryly. "Andy's father is the mayor and he's crazed for publicity. He'd come to the opening of an envelope."

Darcy laughed. "I take it you're not crazy about Andy's dad."

"I don't know," Molly shrugged. "Some people think he's a great mayor, but I have my doubts. For example, there's this organization on the island called C.O.P.E.—it stand for Citizens of Positive Ethics. They're trying to help the poor people who live down in the fishing village. Well, Andy's dad won't give them the time of day. He'd like nothing better than for the world to think there aren't any poor people on Sunset Island."

"I didn't know there were myself until recently," Darcy said with surprise.

"See? I rest my case," Molly answered. "I hear that the mayor is in a really tough reelection fight for the very first time—a young guy, Jerome Paluski, who grew up on the island, is running against him."

"So are your parents backing the mayor?" Darcy asked.

"Absolutely not," Molly said firmly. "They are totally apolitical. It wouldn't surprise me if Jerome Paluski showed up at the party, too."

"Hi, girls!" Caroline called gaily from the doorway. She stepped into the room and pulled out a box wrapped in a red ribbon from behind her back. "For you," she told her daughter, and handed her the box.

"What is it?" Molly asked, opening the gift. She pulled out a cute red shift, with narrow denim straps and denim rickrack on the hem.

"I know red is your favorite color, darling," Molly's mother said eagerly. "Do you like it?"

"It's really nice," Molly said, trying to sound enthusiastic. "Thanks."

"You could wear it to the party!" Caroline suggested.

"I don't want to wear a dress, Mom," Molly said in a low voice. "It's bad enough to know that people will be staring at me in my wheelchair. Why should I put my legs out there on display?"

"I didn't think about that," Caroline admitted. "I'll tell you what, I'll return it and get you a terrific new sweater!"

"You don't have to buy me stuff, Mom," Molly said gently. She wrapped the dress back in the tissue paper, and started to hand it back to her mom. "Hey, wait, I've got a better idea." She looked at Darcy and thrust the box at her. "You take it."

"Me? Oh, I couldn't," Darcy protested.

"Sure, you could," Molly encouraged her. "Mom?"

"It's fine," Caroline assured Darcy. "I think it would look great on you."

"It's really nice of both of you," Darcy said with a laugh, "but in case you didn't notice, I'm about seven inches taller and four sizes bigger than Molly!"

"So? It's a loose-fitting shift!" Molly said. "It might fit you—it'll just be short."

"Go try it on," Caroline urged.

"I really can't—" Darcy began.

"Please?" Molly wheedled. "As a favor to me? I've never seen you in anything except jeans!"

"Okay, I'll try it on," Darcy agreed, heading for Molly's bathroom. "But I'm telling you it'll never fit."

But it did fit. Sure enough, the shift was loose-fitting enough to be one-size-fits-all. The difference was, what would have been roomy on Molly was fitted on Darcy. And it also ended about five inches above her knees. She came out of the bathroom and twirled for Molly and Caroline.

"Hot mama!" Molly cried.

"You look marvelous," Caroline agreed.

"If I bend over, I'll get arrested!" Darcy said, studying herself in front of Molly's full-length mirror.

"I can't believe how great you look!" Molly insisted.

"Oh, come on!" Darcy protested. "I've never worn anything this short in my life!"

"There's a first time for everything," Caroline said grandly. "I vote you wear it. Molly?"

"I second that," Molly agreed. "You're outvoted."

"I bow to the majority," Darcy said, shaking her head.

"Just remember to wear panties," Molly said solemnly.

"Or if you don't wear panties, remember to wear a mask," Caroline suggested with a straight face. "Then we can spread it around that the mask wearer was someone else entirely—we'll pick someone we dislike intensely." She waved good-bye and strode off to get ready for the party.

"Very funny," Darcy laughed. "Listen, I'm going to go hang this up until later—but thanks," she told Molly.

When Darcy hung up the dress in her closet, her eye lit on the antique pale pink camisole that had been her grandmother's—it was one of her very favorite things to wear. Impulsive she pulled it off the hanger and brought it in to Molly. "For you, madam," she said with a flourish, handing Molly the camisole. "It will look *tres* sexy with your jeans tonight."

"Wow, this is beautiful," Molly breathed, fingering the embroidered lace bodice.

"It was Grandma Betty's—my mother's mother," Darcy explained, "from her wedding trousseau."

"I couldn't wear it," Molly said.

"Hey, turnabout is fair play," Darcy insisted. "It'll look mega-hot on you."

"I don't think a girl in a wheelchair can actually qualify as looking mega-hot, no matter what she wears," Molly said softly.

"Bull," Darcy said roughly. She came around in front of Molly and knelt down in front of her chair. "Look, some people are going to stare—okay," Darcy said. "You can slink off or you can face them. You can look drab or you can look hot. It's your choice."

Molly stared at Darcy. "I have a feeling that was one of those motivational speeches that you promised me you'd never make."

"Just wear the stupid camisole," Darcy insisted.

"All right, big shot," Molly replied, a hint of a smile on her lips. "I will."

"Okay, friend, it's party time!" Darcy said as she carried Molly down the stairs and sat her in her wheelchair.

"Onward and upward," Molly murmured.

They'd waited until the gala had been under way for an hour or so—it had been Molly's idea to sort of slip into the crowd. Molly was wearing jeans and the camisole, and she looked darling. Darcy had on the short red shift, and she looked extremely hot. Darcy walked next to Molly as she wheeled her chair around the corner and into the huge interior room the Masons used for parties.

Darcy laughed out loud when she looked around. The room was populated with assorted monsters, ghouls, and ghosts. One man with a bloody hatchet sticking out of his neck was chatting amicably with an Elvira look-alike. A rotund female devil was dancing with dead Elvis—complete with sideburns, jumpsuit, pasty white skin, and ghoulish eyes.

"This is one of the funniest things I've ever seen!" Darcy whispered to Molly.

"I know," Molly whispered back. "It sort of

makes my parents look normal in comparison."

"Beverage?" Simon asked, appearing at Molly's side. He held out a tray full of fluted glasses etched playfully with a skull-and-crossbones motif. "The bloody-looking ones are ginger ale with cherry syrup," Simon explained. "The clear is champagne."

"I'm sticking with the ginger ale," Molly said, grabbing a glass.

"Nothing, thanks," Darcy said. Even the *idea* that the ginger ale was supposed to look bloody made her stomach queasy.

"There's Andy's parents," Molly said, pointing to a couple across the room. He was dressed as Frankenstein, and she was a ghost in a diaphanous white gown.

At that moment Andy's parents spotted Molly, and made their way across the room to join her.

"Molly, we were so sorry to hear about your accident," Andy's mother said in a tremulous voice. She seemed nervous and insecure, and kept looking over at her husband for approval.

"Thanks," Molly responded. She looked over at Darcy. "This is my friend Darcy

Laken. Darcy, this is Mayor Southerby and his wife."

"Nice to meet you," Darcy said.

"It's a terrible tragedy, just terrible," the mayor lamented, taking Molly's hand. "I understand the police haven't got a clue as to who the culprit was who did this to you."

"Right," Molly answered. "There weren't any witnesses, and I just can't remember."

"Really?" the mayor asked sympathetically. "You don't remember a thing about the accident?"

"Actually, some of it is beginning to come back to me," Molly said.

"Really?" the mayor asked sharply. "What sorts of things?"

"Oh, I remember seeing the guy who hit me—even though I still can't remember his face," Molly mumbled, clearly not wanting to talk about it anymore.

"So how is your reelection campaign going?" Darcy asked abruptly, changing the subject.

"Just fine, young lady," the mayor said. "They tell me I've got a fight ahead of me this time, but I like a good fight. Yes, sir!"

"Molly, if there's ever anything we can do—" the mayor's wife began.

"I'm sure Molly's in good hands," the mayor boomed. "Is that son of mine taking good care of you?"

Molly blushed. "Actually, I haven't seen him since the accident."

"What?" the mayor asked, clearly taken aback. "He never mentioned that."

"Oh, Mr. Mayor!" a high-pitched female voice called from across the room. "Do come meet these people!"

"Amy, run ahead and keep that woman from shrieking," the mayor instructed his wife. "I'll be right there."

"Yes, dear, right away," the mayor's wife said nervously, and headed across the room.

"Now, you take care of yourself, Molly," the mayor said, leaning over Molly's wheelchair. "And if there's anything you need from me, you just pick up the phone and call. I'm here to help."

"Thanks," Molly said.

"That's my job; I'm the mayor," he said, and headed across the room to join his wife.

"His wife is afraid of him," Darcy observed, looking across the room at the woman who seemed to shrink in her husband's presence.

"Andy says he's a control freak," Molly

said. "Also a perfectionist. I think maybe Andy's a little afraid of him, too." Molly's face grew sad, thinking about Andy again.

In a way, I know how she feels, Darcy thought. *Even though I'm kind of bummed that Mark Greyson never bothered to call me again, I still think about him sometimes.*

"Listen, we both have guys we need to forget," Darcy said firmly. "There are *definitely* other fish in the sea."

"Speaking of fish," Molly said with a grin, "a big ol' bass just swam into the ballroom."

Darcy looked over and saw Sergeant Scott Phillips standing near the double doors, checking out the crowd. "What's he doing here?" she asked with surprise.

"A few years ago some drunk kids crashed one of our parties," Molly explained. "They broke into some of the cars and stole some purses that were lying around. So now my parents always arrange for security."

"Hi," Scott said, walking over to Molly and Darcy. He had a big grin on his face as he stared appreciatively at Darcy in her red dress. "You look great."

"Thanks," Darcy said. "You look different out of uniform." *Different and hot*, she added to herself. Scott had on faded jeans and a white T-shirt, and he was carrying a worn jeans jacket. The casual clothes emphasized Scott's lean, muscular build.

"I'm here doing security," Scott explained. "Molly's parents didn't want me sticking out like a sore thumb in my blues."

"You would have blended better in a Dracula cape," Molly laughed.

"Molly, honey, come over and say hello to the Packwoods," Gomez said, coming up to his daughter.

"I'd rather stay here in my little corner, Dad," Molly said.

"If anyone is nasty to you, I will bite their neck and suck out all their blood," Gomez promised, and wheeled his daughter across the room.

"Interesting man," Scott said.

"Unique," Darcy added.

"They aren't for real, are they?" Scott asked.

"No one knows," Darcy replied, wiggling her eyebrows in a sinister fashion.

Scott laughed. "I'm really glad to see you again," Scott said in a low voice.

"Me, too," Darcy admitted.

"Really?" Scott asked, his face lighting up. "I thought about calling you, but I've been working on this brutal case that just wrapped up this morning—a really rough one."

"Maybe now you'll have even more time for Molly's case," Darcy said pointedly.

"Hey, you can't imagine how badly I'd like to catch that guy, Darcy," Scott said firmly.

"Well, it would help if you believed what I told you about the guy in the green sports car," Darcy said.

Scott sighed. "Look, I believe that *you* believe it's true, but I just can't swallow that psychic stuff!"

"Did you have any luck tracing the car?" Darcy asked, trying to control her irritation.

"Nope," Scott said earnestly. "And believe me, I have been looking."

"I believe you," Darcy murmured.

"Has Molly remembered anything else about her accident?"

"No," Darcy said. "I'm torn between wishing she'd remember so we could catch the lowlife, and not wanting her to remember because it's so painful for her."

"Yeah, I see your point," Scott said. "But look, if she remembers anything—I mean anything at all—be sure to call me immediately, okay?"

"Okay," Darcy agreed. She was touched by the firmness of his voice—evidently he wanted to catch the criminal as badly as she did. "Thanks," she added, putting her hand lightly on Scott's arm.

And then pulled it away quickly, as if she'd been burnt.

Because in that brief moment, touching Scott's arm, she'd felt something terrible: evil, horror, death.

Darcy took a step backward and stared at Scott. At Scott's sandy blond hair.

The same color hair as the man Molly remembered leaning over her after the accident, the same color hair as the man in the green car.

TWELVE

"Darcy, what is it?" Scott asked with concern. "Are you okay?" He took a step forward and reached out for her.

"I'm fine," she said, quickly stepping back, out of his reach.

"You look so pale. Are you sure you're okay?"

"Yes, yes," Darcy assured him faintly. "I . . . I just need to go . . . talk to Molly. Excuse me." With her heart pounding in her chest, she turned and scanned the crowded room, searching for her friend. She saw her sitting in her wheelchair on the far side of the room, talking with a monster whose face dripped blood, and a giant lizard with fangs.

"Molly, hi," Darcy said, quickly walking over to her.

"Hi," Molly said, looking relieved to see Darcy. "What's up?"

"Oh, nothing," Darcy said, trying to sound casual. She hadn't figured out what to do yet, or how to handle this.

"We just think you're so brave, Molly," the lizard mouthed.

"Such an inspiration," the monster agreed.

"You know, the mind is very powerful," the lizard continued, waving around an unlizardlike manicured hand festooned with ostentatious diamond rings. "Have you thought about how you might have attracted this turn of events to occur?"

"Gee, no," Molly said, feigning innocence. "But I bet you'll explain it."

"What Buffy means is that perhaps there was some lesson you needed to learn from your Higher Power," the monster said earnestly. "If you learn it, who knows what will happen!"

"Right!" Buffy-the-lizard agreed, taking a voracious bite of wheat cracker and pâté. "I heard there was a man in New York who thought so positively, he cured himself of AIDS."

Darcy saw the look on Molly's face, a look that said she was about to push the lizard's face into her pâté, and she quickly looked at her watch. "Gee, would you look at the time! she said loudly. "Molly, we promised we'd go to that thing."

"Thing?" Molly echoed, still seething in the direction of her companions.

"Yes, you know, the *thing*," Darcy repeated, hoping that Molly would pick up on the fact that she was trying to help her make a smooth getaway.

"Oh, right!" Molly agreed, getting Darcy's intention. "The *thing*!" She turned back to the lizard and the monster. "We're going to hold a satanic ritual up in my bedroom," she told them confidentially. "I figure if I sacrifice enough small animals, the devil will fix my legs. 'Bye!"

Darcy and Molly both waved a perky good-bye, leaving the monster and the lizard with their mouths hanging open in shock.

"Thank you for rescuing me," Molly said, when they reached the kitchen. "I've sparkled about all I can for one night. Let's go upstairs."

"Are you sure?" Darcy asked. She was filled with anxiety. *If I'm alone with Molly,* Darcy thought anxiously, *I'm going to tell her the entire truth. She's got to know about*

Scott! We've got to do something! But what if she hates me for not telling her I knew she'd have the accident? I couldn't bear it. . . .

"Yeah," Molly answered. "I really want out of here."

"You got it, then." Darcy lifted Molly and carried her up the winding stairs.

"Ah, privacy at last," Molly said, stretching out on her bed. "Hey, if you want to go back down and hang out with Scott, it's fine with me."

"No!" Darcy said forcefully.

"It's okay, honest," Molly told her with a smile. "I saw the way he was looking at you."

"What way?" Darcy asked, alarmed.

Molly gave her a funny look. "Like he thinks you're hot, dummy!"

Darcy stared at Molly a moment, then turned and began pacing the room. "I . . . I have to talk to you about something," she began.

"So talk," Molly said.

"It's not so easy," Darcy said, pacing even more rapidly.

"Look, quit wearing out my carpet; you're making me nuts!" Molly said. "Just sit down and talk to me."

Darcy sat on the edge of Molly's bed. "I don't know where to begin," she said softly.

"Wow, you really look upset," Molly answered. "It can't be that bad."

"Yes, it can." Darcy took a deep breath and shut her eyes. "There's something about me I never told you. I should have, but I didn't."

"Let me guess," Molly mused. "You really *do* sacrifice small animals to the Prince of Darkness. No? How about—Buffy, the Lizard Woman, is your evil twin sister. Or, wait, I've got it! You've got every album Barry Manilow ever recorded!"

"Molly, I'm serious!"

"Okay, I'll be serious, then," Molly said softly. She looked at Darcy expectantly.

"Ever since I was a little girl," Darcy began, "I've been able to do this weird thing. Sometimes . . . well, sometimes I just *know* things."

"Go on," Molly urged.

"Sometimes it happens in a dream, sometimes in a flash while I'm awake," Darcy continued. "When I was just a kid I knew there was going to be a fire in our house right before it happened, and I was right. Once my mom's friend Bertie was going on a train trip to visit her sister, and the night before she was leaving, I dreamt that her train would crash, and it did."

"Have you ever thought about a career in Vegas?" Molly quipped. "Or how about we go pick a few lottery numbers!"

"I'm telling you the truth," Darcy said quietly.

Molly looked at her closely. "You really are, aren't you?" she realized.

"This . . . this thing that happens to me," Darcy said, "I don't have any control over it. Sometimes it happens often—twice in one week, maybe—and sometimes months and months will go by without anything."

Molly nodded, staring intently at her friend.

"Well, right before I met you, I was at my high school graduation, and a really awful thing happened." Darcy told Molly the whole story about how she'd seen a tumor in Marianne's brain, and then how Marianne had had a physical that showed she was in perfect health.

"Maybe she's going to get a tumor in the future," Molly suggested. "Can psychic stuff work like that?"

"My dad said the same thing," Darcy replied. "And the answer is, I don't know. But the terrible thing is, it's the first time that I *knew* something, and it turned out to be false. It really threw me—how could I ever trust my own instincts again? I've never been very comfortable with this, anyway," Darcy explained. "You know me; I'm not a real airy-fairy kind of person!"

"That's exactly why I do believe you," Molly said. "You're not the kind of person to ever make this up."

"Well, thanks for that," Darcy said.

"So is that what you had to tell me?"

"There's more," Darcy said in a low voice. *Okay, Darcy, this is it,* she told herself. *You've got to do it. But please, God, don't let her hate me.* "The night before your accident, I had a terrible nightmare that you were going to be in a car wreck," Darcy confessed, "but . . . after what happened with Marianne, I didn't trust myself anymore."

"You . . . you knew?" Molly whispered, her face quickly going a ghostly white.

"I didn't think I knew; I didn't believe it!" Darcy tried to explain. "I tried to call you the next morning, but you weren't home. And after that, I put it out of my mind until I called you that night, but by then it was too late!" Tears were running down Darcy's cheeks. How could Molly forgive her? She could never forgive herself.

"I don't know what to say," Molly gulped. "You knew. . . ."

"Oh, Molly, please try to understand, I didn't *know* I knew! I'm so sorry! I'd do anything in the world to change what happened, if I only could!" Darcy cried.

Molly put a trembling hand over her mouth. "I need to be alone right now," she whispered.

"But there's more that I have to tell you—"

"No," Molly interrupted. "You have to go. I can't look at you right now."

"Okay. I understand," Darcy managed between sobs. She got up and walked out the door.

She hates me, and I don't blame her, Darcy thought as she sat on her bed, crying and rocking back and forth. *I'll never be able to forgive myself. Never.* Darcy cried until she felt empty and exhausted. She fell back on her bed and stared at the ceiling, trying to figure out a plan. *I might as well pack while I'm planning,* she told herself miserably. *It's pretty clear that Molly never wants to see me again.*

"What am I going to do about Scott?" she said out loud as she pulled her suitcase out of the closet. *I can't very well go to the police—he* is *the police!* she thought. *Besides, what would I tell them? Arrest Sergeant Scott Phillips because I say so? They'll think I'm crazy!*

By the time Darcy had emptied her drawers into her suitcase, she'd come to a conclusion. She would have to try to get some proof that Scott was guilty herself. It was the only way. And it was the least she could do for Molly.

By the time Darcy left her room, it was very late. She tiptoed down the hall with her suitcase in hand, and peeked into Molly's room. The lights were off, and it appeared that Molly was fast asleep. Downstairs, everything was quiet and dark, the party long over. Darcy put the note she'd written to Mr. and Mrs. Mason on the table in the foyer, and took one last look around the strange and wonderful mansion, eerily illuminated by the light of the moon streaming in through the front windows.

"Good-bye," Darcy said softly. "I'm sorry."

She closed the front door behind her and walked out the door.

Because of the full moon, Darcy was able to see somewhat as she trudged down the private road. Her plan was to walk to the ferry station—she figured it was about five miles—and to nap there until the first ferry arrived. She knew it was already almost three o'clock in the morning, and the first ferry left at six.

Downward she climbed, stumbling occasionally over an unexpected rut in the dirt road, lost in morose thought. *Maybe if I'd told Molly the truth before I ever accepted the job, it would have been better*, Darcy thought guiltily. But deep down, she knew nothing really mattered except that she hadn't intervened before the accident, when she'd had the chance.

What was that? Darcy stopped, listening carefully. She was certain she'd heard a noise. *Probably just a small animal*, she decided. That reminded her of the joke she'd shared with Molly just hours before, about sacrificing small animals, and total misery overtook her. Everything was just so awful.

Crack! She heard it again! Darcy stood stock-still, every fiber of her body straining to hear. She stared into the woods on either side of the road, which now seemed full of menace. *Crack!* Suddenly, out of the darkness, a figure seemed to jump in front of her.

It was Scott.

Silence.

"Darcy!" Scott finally said. "What the hell are you doing out here?"

"I was about to ask you the same thing," Darcy said, trying to keep her voice level. *Don't let on that you're scared*, she warned herself frantically.

Scott held his flashlight under his chin, giving his face a sinister cast. "Don't you know it's dangerous, walking around by yourself in the woods?" he asked.

"I can take care of myself," Darcy assured him in what she hoped was a confident-sounding voice. She put down her suitcase, prepared to make a run for it if she had to. "You didn't answer my question. What are you doing here?"

"I was making my last rounds, driving by the grounds," Scott said, "and I thought I saw someone running away from the house, so I parked the car and followed them."

Yeah, right. "Did you find them?" Darcy asked.

"No," Scott answered. Slowly he moved the flashlight until it shone on Darcy's face. "Where are you going?" he asked softly.

Darcy squinted and turned her head from the light. "Home. I got a call from my dad. He's . . . he's not feeling well, and he asked me to come home."

"In the middle of the night?" Scott asked.

"Yes," Darcy replied. "Get that flashlight out of my face," she snapped.

Scott turned the flashlight out. Now their faces were illuminated by the ghostly light from the full moon. "Why don't you take the van?"

"I didn't want to wake anyone up to ask permission," Darcy said.

"Didn't your father's call wake them up?" Scott asked.

"Look, I don't have to stand here and answer your questions. I've got to go." Darcy picked up her suitcase again, prepared to bluff her way through.

"No need to walk, Darcy," Scott said. "Come on back and get in my car, and I'll drive you to the ferry."

"No, thanks," Darcy said.

"Don't be ridiculous," Scott said. He stepped forward and reached out his hand.

He's going to touch me! Darcy thought frantically. But he didn't. He simply reached for her suitcase, and started back up the hill.

What do I do now! Darcy thought desperately. *If I run away, he can catch me. Maybe if I just play along, pretend everything is normal, nothing will happen. After all, he doesn't know that I know. I'll walk back to the house with him, and instead of getting in his car, I'll run inside. That's what I'll do.*

But as they got closer to the house, Darcy realized with a sinking heart that Scott's car was parked in a little side spot, and not up at the house at all. She knew she was still too far away to be heard if she screamed. *I've got to figure out what to do*, Darcy thought wildly, trying to look composed as they approached the car. She was surprised to see that it wasn't a police car, but was, in fact, Scott's personal vehicle.

A green sports car.

Like a shot Darcy took off down the road, sprinting as fast as her legs would carry her.

"Darcy! What the hell . . . ?" Scott was screaming.

But she kept running, frantically forcing her legs to pump harder, and harder still. She realized that she had thoughtlessly begun to run down the hill toward the road, instead of toward the house. The road was a longer distance, and didn't guarantee any safety. But she hadn't had a moment to think, and now her course had already been decided.

Stumbling once, she righted herself, listening for Scott's approaching footsteps. *As soon as I hear him, I'll duck into the woods*, she decided, and ran even harder. But all she heard was the sound of her own panicked breath.

Until she heard the car.

Scott had gotten into the car, and was now driving it crazily down the road. Darcy saw the headlights careening off the rocks, and she willed herself to go faster. But there was no way she could outrun him. She was almost to the main road. *What should I do? I'm scared!* she wanted to scream.

Just before she got to the road, with the car bearing down on her, she darted into the woods, praying she could somehow find her way forward in the dense foliage.

She heard Scott stop, and get out of his car. Now she could hear him rustling through the trees, following her. For a moment his flashlight caught her, and she stood, unable to move, like a fawn caught in his headlights. *Run!* she told herself, and propelled herself forward once again, dodging crazily through the woods, branches breaking, sharp thorns tearing at her arms.

Almost there! Almost to the road! Up ahead she could see just the edge of a clearing and she careened headlong toward it, hoping against hope that a car would come by, that someone would please, please, save her.

There was a car in the clearing! There was someone to rescue her! Darcy ran toward the car, not caring if it was two kids making out, not caring who it was parked in the middle of the night, just so thankful that someone was there.

Then she stopped. Because it was a Jaguar. A green Jaguar. And inside was a man with blond hair.

And Darcy knew.

This was the car that had tried to run the van off the road. She shut her eyes, and realized that Scott's car wasn't even a Jaguar—and Scott's car was old and beat-up. How could she have made such a stupid mistake?

The car door opened, and the man with the

blond hair started to get out, an insane look in his eyes. Just at that moment, Scott ran out of the woods and into the clearing. "Darcy! Are you crazy! What the hell—" And then Scott saw the blond guy, and the green Jaguar, and he stopped dead in his tracks.

When the blond man saw that Darcy wasn't alone, he shot her a look of panic, then scrambled back into his car. He quickly turned it on, and tore off with a squeal of his tires.

"That's him!" Darcy screamed. "That's the guy who tried to run us off the road! We've got to catch him!"

"By the time we get back to my car, he'll be far, far away," Scott said.

"Well, we've got to try!" Darcy insisted.

"It doesn't matter," Scott says. "I saw his face. I know who he is."

"You do?" Darcy asked in complete surprise. "Who?"

"That's the mayor's son," Scott said. "That's Andy Southerby."

THIRTEEN

"Okay, now do you want to tell me what the hell is going on?" Scott asked Darcy. They had walked back to Scott's car, and now sat in the darkness. Darcy felt so numb from all the events of the last few hours that she'd been unable to say a word on the walk back to the car.

"I messed everything up," Darcy moaned, letting her head fall back on the headrest.

"Look, berate yourself later, give me some facts now," Scott said tersely.

Darcy turned to him, barely making out his face in the dark. "I'm so sorry, Scott. I . . . I thought it was you!"

"You *what?*" Scott asked incredulously.

"I touched you at the party, and got this terrible feeling, and then you showed up out of nowhere on the road, and then when I saw your car—"

"Darcy," Scott interrupted. "You are babbling. Start from the beginning, like why you suddenly ran away from me during the party and never came back."

"Okay," Darcy said. She took a deep breath and told Scott the whole story, from what she'd felt when she touched his arm at the party, to telling Molly that she'd had a premonition about her accident, and right through to running into the blond man—whom she now knew to be Andy Southerby.

"Wow," Scott breathed, shaking his head ruefully. "What a night." He draped his arm along the back of the seat and gently touched Darcy's hair. "Feel anything?"

"No," she said softly.

He reached under her hair and ever-so-lightly touched the back of her neck. "Feel anything now?"

"No," she admitted.

Slowly his fingers stroked the back of her neck, until she felt some of the tension ebbing away. She closed her eyes and leaned back against his hand.

"Feel anything now?" he asked.

"I feel something, but it's not bad," she said, a slight smile on her face.

"I don't know why that happened when you touched me at the party," Scott said, "but I've got a theory. Remember I told you I'd just finished working on a really tough, gruesome case? Well, it was a woman who was battered by her husband. She was still alive when we got there, and she died in my arms."

"Oh, God, Scott, that's horrible!"

"Yeah," Scott agreed gruffly. "And I'm thinking maybe that's what you picked up on."

Darcy lifted her head and looked at him. "Hey, that means you believe me about my premonitions!"

"Not necessarily—" Scott began.

"Yes, you do; you're just so freaked out that it isn't in your rule book that you can't admit to it!" Darcy said.

"What I believe is immaterial," Scott said. "Let's deal with facts. You just ID'd the mayor's son as the guy who tried to run you off the road."

"Which is the same guy who hit Molly and then ran away," Darcy said adamantly.

"That is not fact," Scott told her.

"It is in my book," came Darcy's retort. "So what do we do now? Put out an all-points bulletin?"

Scott smiled. "You've seen too many cop shows. We have to proceed very carefully here. You are talking about the son of the most important man on Sunset Island."

"Who cares?" Darcy asked. "A criminal is a criminal!"

"Darcy, use your brains," Scott admonished. "Chase Southerby and the Chief of Police are best friends. If I put an APB out on Andy, my butt would be in a sling. Besides, we don't have enough evidence. And you told me yourself when you reported the incident that you couldn't see the driver very well."

"Then we'll get the evidence!" Darcy cried. "Let's go to the mayor's mansion and see if Andy's there!"

"Not so fast, hotshot," Scott said. "First we wait until a decent hour—I don't know about you, but I need a few hours of sleep. Then I'll pay a visit to Andy and very politely ask him a few questions."

"And then?" Darcy asked impatiently.

"And then I'll figure out my next move," Scott replied.

"Oh, no you don't, bucko," Darcy said, turning in the seat to face Scott fully. "I'm not getting left out of this. I'm going with you."

"Darcy, you aren't a police officer—"

"Too bad!" Darcy flared. "Can you even imagine how I feel, when I knew about Molly's accident and didn't warn her in time? You have to let me be a part of catching Andy! Besides, if I'm there, maybe I'll get a psychic flash that will help."

Scott groaned. "It's against everything in my rule book—"

Darcy looked at him with flashing eyes. "Well, then," she said archly, "I suggest you leave your rule book at home."

"Darcy? Is that you?" Molly whispered as Darcy was tiptoeing by her door.

"Yeah," Darcy answered reluctantly, putting down her suitcase. She had agreed with Scott that her best plan was to sneak back into the Mason's house as if she'd never left, and then get up early to pay a visit to Andy Southerby. It hadn't been difficult to sneak back into the house, but now she'd awakened Molly trying to get past her room.

"Come on in," Molly said. "I called you through the intercom a million times, but you never answered. Did you leave?"

"I started to," Darcy admitted, sitting on the foot of Molly's bed.

"What made you come back?"

"It's a long story," Darcy replied with a sigh. "Anyway, I'm sorry I woke you, and I'll leave in the morning, I promise."

"Oh, Darcy, I don't want you to leave!" Molly cried.

Darcy stared at her incredulously. "You don't?"

"No, of course not! How could you assume that and not even talk to me about it?"

"I'm sorry," Darcy said honestly. "I really thought you never wanted to see my face again!"

"Darcy, I was in shock! I mean, there you were, telling me that you'd had a premonition about my accident, that if I'd only known, I might not be stuck in a wheelchair for the rest of my life."

"I'm so sorry!"

"But, Darcy, you *did* try to call me! You told me so yourself!"

"Well, yes," Darcy said hesitantly, "but I

should have tried harder to track you down. . . ."

"You know, since the accident, I've had a lot of time to think. I don't know how the universe works. No one knows."

"But I knew that—"

"You didn't *know*," Molly said firmly. "You had a dream. Maybe even if you'd told me about your dream before my accident, the same thing would have happened. I wouldn't have stayed locked in my room for the rest of my life, now would I?"

"I guess not," Darcy said softly.

"I mean, think about it, Darcy, do you really believe that you have the ability to change the course of events, to change people's lives?"

"I don't know!" Darcy cried tearfully. "That's what's so hard about having this bizarre ability. I don't know how it all works!"

"No one knows," Molly said firmly. She looked down and pulled a loose thread out of her quilt. "I wish more than anything in this world that I could still walk." She looked up at Darcy. "Did I ever tell you that in my dreams, my legs are fine? I can run, dance, anything!"

"No," Darcy said over the lump in her throat.

"It makes sleeping fun," Molly said with a small smile. She was quiet for a moment, searching for the right words. "None of my wishes or prayers are going to change what happened. But . . . having you here, well, it makes it bearable. Almost, anyway. I . . . I don't have to pretend around you. I can just be myself. You're the best friend I ever had."

Wordlessly Darcy scooted up the bed and put her arms around Molly, tears streaming down her face. "You're one of the best friends I've ever had, too," she said. "Believe me, you probably help me even more than I help you."

"I hope so," Molly said, fighting to laugh through her tears, "because Lord knows you need a lot of help!"

Darcy laughed and plucked a couple of tissues from the box on the nightstand. She handed one to Molly, then blew her own nose. "Before we get too bogged down in this love-fest, I've got to tell you what happened to me tonight. It's going to sound unbelievable, but here goes." And then Darcy told Molly everything.

"Andy?" Molly asked in shock when Darcy had finished. "Come on, that's ridiculous!"

"But it's true!" Darcy insisted.

"I would have recognized him when he leaned over me at the accident!" Molly protested.

"You said yourself you couldn't really make out the person's face because something was in your eyes, and you were in shock!"

"But . . . why? Why would Andy do this? It doesn't make any sense!"

"Well, that's what we have to find out," Darcy said firmly.

Molly shook her head. "I just can't swallow this. Andy is my . . ." She began, but she let the rest of the sentence dangle in the air.

"He's never spoken to you once since the accident," Darcy said gently. "He's never come to visit. You have to admit, that's strange."

"Maybe . . ." Molly said in a quavering voice.

"I'm meeting Scott downstairs at eight o'clock," Darcy said. "We're going over to the mayor's mansion to talk to Andy, if he's there."

"And if he's not?" Molly asked.

"Then we'll find him," Darcy replied, steely-voiced. "No matter what it takes, I'm going to find him."

FOURTEEN

"You've got to promise me that you'll let me do all the talking," Scott said as he drove the car toward the mayor's mansion later that morning.

"What if you miss something?" Darcy asked.

"I won't!" Scott replied.

"But what if you do?" Darcy insisted. "I'm just supposed to stand there like my IQ dropped thirty points?"

"You are really infuriating!" Scott exploded. "Do you know the kind of trouble I could get into for even bringing you along on this little adventure?"

"Okay, okay," Darcy said. "I'll keep my mouth shut—unless you mess up in a really major way."

"Gee, thanks," Scott murmured sarcastically. They drove along in silence for a while, until finally Scott broke down. "Look, we're both just tired—two hours of sleep just doesn't make it. Truce?"

"Truce," Darcy agreed, lightly touching him on the arm. She was happy to find that all she felt was the pleasant sensation of being attracted to him. *I'd like to touch more than his arm, actually,* she thought lasciviously. *Now, stop that, Darcy! That is totally inappropriate! You are here on serious police business.*

"Whoa, nice little shack," Darcy marveled as they drove up to the formidable-looking mansion. "This looks like something straight out of *Gone With the Wind.*"

"The Southerbys are very wealthy, and very influential," Scott said as he parked in the circular driveway. He turned and gave Darcy a sharp look. "This has to be handled with kid gloves, or the whole thing will blow up in my face."

"Gotcha," Darcy said, nodding seriously.

"Here goes," Scott said, getting out of the car. He rang the bell at the front door, making a gesture to Darcy that reminded her to keep her lip zipped.

"Why, Scott, what are you doing here?"

Amy Southerby asked, nervously fingering the pearls around her neck. "The butler is off today, and I saw you drive up."

"Good morning, Mrs. Southerby," Scott said, taking off his hat respectfully. "Sorry to stop by unannounced. I hope I'm not disturbing you."

"No, not at all," Mrs. Southerby said, but Darcy couldn't help but notice how nervous she seemed.

"I was wondering if Andy was home," Scott said.

"Andy? What do you want with Andy?" Mrs. Southerby looked from Scott to Darcy, then back to Scott again.

"I'd just like to ask him a few questions, ma'am," Scott said.

"He's not here," the mayor said, coming up suddenly behind his wife. "He went to Portland to visit a friend."

"Can you tell me when he left, sir?" Scott asked the mayor.

"He's been there all week, as a matter of fact," the mayor said. "Hasn't he, Amy?"

"Uh, yes," Mrs. Southerby agreed, her eyes darting away from her husband.

"I demand to know what this is all about," the mayor ordered.

As Scott explained that he just needed to ask Andy a few questions about a report of wreckless driving—which Scott was sure was a case of mistaken identity—Darcy kept her eyes on Mrs. Southerby. Her eyes kept darting toward the side of the house. As Scott and the mayor continued talking, Darcy casually took a few steps backward, until she could see the outside of the house on the right-hand side. Nothing looked amiss.

And then she saw him.

Andy was sneaking stealthily out of a side door, running toward an auxiliary garage perhaps five hundred feet away.

"It's Andy!" Darcy screamed, and like a flash she took off after him. Pumping as hard as she could, she managed to reach him just as he was about to get into his car.

"Hey, not so fast!" she yelled, spinning him around.

Andy pivoted, pulled back his fist, and punched Darcy in the jaw. Then he jumped into his car and peeled off.

"Are you okay?" Scott asked, running up to her. He helped her to her feet.

"Let's go get the bastard," was all Darcy said, and she took off toward Scott's car.

"Faster!" Darcy yelled as they sped around a sharp curve, keeping Andy's car in their sights.

"I don't plan to get us killed," Scott yelled, keeping his eyes on the road. "Dead Man's Curve is coming up. If he takes it that fast, he'll never make it."

Andy's car came around the bend and headed into the dangerous curve. For a moment, he seemed to lose control of the car, then he pulled the steering wheel sharply, and the car spun in a circle and died. Desperately Andy tried to start it again, but it was useless. Scott pulled up next to him with a squeal of his tires.

Andy jumped out of the car and ran down the steep ravine, twisting and then tumbling, righting himself to run again. Darcy and Scott were hot after him. Scott stumbled, but Darcy's years of perfecting her balance on a diving board gave her an edge, and she deftly moved closer to her prey. Andy stumbled again, and just as he was getting up, Darcy caught him by the collar of his shirt. She grabbed his arm and pinned it hard behind his back. Scott arrived just a second later.

"What took you so long?" Darcy panted.

"I didn't do anything!" Andy screamed, struggling against Darcy.

"Let him go, Darcy," Scott said, pulling out his handcuffs.

"You haven't got anything on me!" Andy yelled. "My father will cremate you!"

"Running from a police officer is a criminal offense," Scott said, putting the handcuffs on Andy. "And your father was obviously covering for you. You should have told him about last night, so at least he could get his story straight. You have the right to remain silent. You have the right to an attorney—"

"Just one moment, please, before you officially arrest him," Darcy said pleasantly. She turned to Andy, pulled back her fist, and decked him. "Nobody punches Darcy Laken and gets away with it," she told a stunned Andy. "Nobody."

"You can't do that!" Scott hissed at Darcy.

"I already did!"

But Andy was paying no attention. Suddenly all the fight seemed to go out of him. He put his head on his knees and wept. "God, I'm so sorry," he sobbed. "I never meant to hurt her!"

Scott helped him to his feet. "You don't

have to tell me anything, Andy, until you have an attorney present."

"How could you do it?" Darcy asked him. "How could you hit Molly's car and then run away?"

"You don't have to say anything—" Scott began, apparently afraid Darcy might corrupt the arrest.

"I didn't hit her," Andy sobbed. "As God is my witness, I didn't do it!"

"Get off it!" Darcy demanded. "It was you that she remembers bending over her, crying, wasn't it?"

"That was me," Andy said with a shudder. "I was in the car that hit her, but I wasn't driving."

"Who was?" Darcy asked.

"My dad," Andy whispered. "It was my dad."

"I just can't believe it," Molly said flatly. It was a few hours later, and Darcy had just returned from the police station and told her the whole story about Andy and his father.

"But it's true," Darcy insisted. "Andy made a full confession. His dad was driving the car. It was just a horrible freak accident—they didn't even realize it was you at first! Andy ran out of the car to come see if you were okay, then his dad forced him to get back in the car, into the driver's seat, in case anybody saw them."

"You mean the mayor just left me to bleed to death, and would have let Andy take the blame if I'd remembered anything or if anyone had witnessed the accident?"

"Yeah, some lowlife, huh?" Darcy said. "The mayor thought it would ruin his political career if it got out, so he was willing to foist the blame off on his kid. I guess Andy is just so afraid of his dad, he was willing to agree. His father promised him that if he did get caught, he'd make sure he never went to jail; he'd get off with probation."

"But what about Andy trying to force our van off the road?" Molly asked.

"That really was Andy, all right," Darcy said. "I think he just lost it. He says originally he had driven over to see you, but he couldn't bring himself to face you, so he parked by the bottom of the private road and just sat there, brooding. But he had heard from Jenny that you'd had a memory of someone bending over you while you were lying on the ground—I told Jenny and Rowena about it when they came to visit you. So he got really scared," Darcy said with a shrug. "He didn't want to take the blame, but he couldn't bring himself to turn his dad in. . . ."

"So he tried to run us off the road, instead," Molly said bitterly. "He tried to kill me."

"A dead woman's memory can't come back," Darcy said grimly.

Molly was silent for a moment. "How could I have been so wrong about him?" she whispered.

"Don't be too hard on yourself," Darcy said gently. "Andy fooled a lot of people."

Molly sighed and stared wistfully out the window. "Do you think I'll ever have another boyfriend?"

"Absolutely," Darcy said firmly. "You are one incredible girl."

"So . . . is Scott going to arrest the mayor?" Molly asked.

"He's probably doing that even as we speak," Darcy said with satisfaction.

Molly gave Darcy a wan smile. "You are really something. Have you ever considered a career as a detective?"

"No," Darcy laughed. "Do you think I should?"

"I have a feeling you'd be brilliant," Molly mused. "That is, if you could manage to finish an investigation before you stepped in and threw a punch at the poor guy you were investigating!"

"I'll try to remember that," Darcy said, stretching out her back. "Man, I'm beat. I need a hot shower and a long nap. Can you fend for yourself for a few hours?"

"Sure," Molly replied.

"Okay, well, catch you later," Darcy called, heading out of Molly's room.

"Hey, wait a sec!" Molly yelled. Darcy stuck her head back in. "Do you mind if I thank you, you wild woman, you?"

"No," Darcy said quietly. "And you're welcome."

"I have to thank Scott, too."

"Did I mention that he's coming over later tonight with a half gallon of chocolate-chocolate chip ice cream from Sweet Stuff? Lucky you!"

Molly laughed. "You mean lucky *you!*"

Darcy walked back into Molly's room and sat next to her on her bed. "You're right, Molly. Lucky me. Thanks for being my friend."

"Ditto," Molly said softly. "You're one of a

kind, Darcy Laken, which is probably a good thing—two of you would be dangerous!"

"Yeah, but two of *us* is perfect," Darcy said, hugging her friend tight. "We're going to have zillions of incredible adventures!"

Molly frowned. "You mean I'm not spending my life in my room pining for what might have been?"

"Not a chance," Darcy replied. "By the way, I understand that there's a program to teach paraplegics to parachute-jump," she added nonchalantly.

"Oh, really?" Molly said. "And just how do you happen to understand that?"

"Oh, I might have made a few phone calls," Darcy said innocently, "and they might have said they'll send you some literature in the mail."

"Hey, wait a minute—" Molly protested.

"I'm wiped out, gotta run," Darcy said, springing to the door.

"I'm not doing it!" Molly yelled.

"Oh, yes you are!" Darcy yelled back.

And as Darcy bopped down to her room with a huge grin on her face, she knew that on the other side of the wall, Molly's shining face matched hers.

GET PSYCHED FOR ALL-NEW ADVENTURES ON SUNSET ISLAND!

Darcy Laken is a beautiful, street-smart eighteen-year-old befriended by Emma, Carrie, and Sam in *Sunset Scandal*. She lives on the *other* side of Sunset Island—in an old and foreboding house on a hill where she works for the eccentric Mason family. When Darcy and Molly Mason find themselves in danger, Darcy gets a premonition about who is responsible. But when she asks for help from the cute guy who is threatening to steal her heart, he doesn't believe her!

DON'T MISS A SINGLE ADVENTURE FEATURING DARCY!

__SUNSET AFTER DARK   0-425-13772-4/$3.50

__SUNSET AFTER MIDNIGHT 0-425-13799-6/$3.50
(Coming in April)

__SUNSET AFTER HOURS   0-425-13666-3/$3.50
(Coming in May)

Sam, Carrie, and Emma return to Sunset Island and their summer jobs as au pairs...
Let the adventure begin!

By Cherie Bennett

___*SUNSET HEAT #7*___   **0-425-13383-4/$3.99**

Sam is hired by a talent scout to dance in a show in Japan. Unfortunately, Emma and Carrie don't share her enthusiasm. No one really knows if this is on the up and up, especially after her fiasco with the shifty photographer last summer. But Sam is determined to go despite her friends. . .

___*SUNSET PROMISES #8*___   **0-425-13384-2/$3.50**

Carrie receives a lot of attention when she shows her photos at the Sunset Gallery. She is approached by a publisher who wants her to do a book of pictures of the island. But when Carrie photos the entire island, she discovers a part of Sunset Island that tourists never see...

___*SUNSET SCANDAL #9*___   **0-425-13385-0/$3.50**

Emma has started to see Kurt again, and everything's going great...until Kurt is arrested as the suspect in a rash of robberies! He has no alibi, and things look pretty bad. Then, Emma befriends a new girl on the island who might be able to help prove Kurt's innocence.

___*SUNSET WHISPERS #10*___   **0-425-13386-9/$3.50**

Sam is shocked to find out she is adopted. She's never needed her friends more than when her birth mother comes to Sunset Island to meet her. And to add to the chaos, Sam and Emma, along with the rest of the girls on the island, are auditioning to be back up in the rock band *Flirting with Danger*.

For Visa, MasterCard and American Express orders ($15 minimum) call: **1-800-631-8571**

FOR MAIL ORDERS: CHECK BOOK(S). FILL OUT COUPON. SEND TO:	**POSTAGE AND HANDLING:** $1.75 for one book, 75¢ for each additional. Do not exceed $5.50.
BERKLEY PUBLISHING GROUP 390 Murray Hill Pkwy., Dept. B East Rutherford, NJ 07073	**BOOK TOTAL** $ ____
NAME_____	**POSTAGE & HANDLING** $ ____
ADDRESS _____	**APPLICABLE SALES TAX** $ ____ (CA, NJ, NY, PA)
CITY_____	**TOTAL AMOUNT DUE** $ ____
STATE_____ ZIP_____	**PAYABLE IN US FUNDS.**
PLEASE ALLOW 6 WEEKS FOR DELIVERY. PRICES ARE SUBJECT TO CHANGE WITHOUT NOTICE.	(No cash orders accepted.)